# On Poetry
# and
# Poets

# On Poetry and Poets

## Selected Essays of A. J. M. Smith

With an Introduction by the Author
General Editor: Malcolm Ross

New Canadian Library No. 143

McClelland and Stewart

*The Canadian Publishers*
McClelland and Stewart Limited
25 Hollinger Road
Toronto, Ontario

Printed and bound in Canada

# Contents

# Sources

"Canadian Anthologies, New and Old," *University of Toronto Quarterly*, XI. 4, July, 1942, pp. 457-474.

"Introduction" to The Book of Canadian Poetry, 1st ed. Chicago: University of Chicago Press, 1943, pp. 3-31.

"Reviews of Books," *Canadian Historical Review*, XXV, 2, June, 1944, pp. 196-199.

"The Poetry of Duncan Campbell Scott," *Dalhousie Review*, XXVIII, 1, April, 1948, pp. 12-21.

"Refining Fire: The Meaning and Use of Poetry," *Queen's Quarterly*, LXI, Autumn, 1954, pp. 353-364.

"The Recent Poetry of Irving Layton: A Major Voice," *Queen's Quarterly*, LXII, 4, Winter, 1955-56, pp. 587-591.

"Introduction" to *The Blasted Pine*, 1st ed. Toronto, Macmillan 1957, pp. xv-xix.

"A Garland for E. J. Pratt," *Table Ronde*, No. 6, Winter, 1958, pp. 66-71.

"Book Reviews," *Dalhousie Review*, Vol. 71, 1974, pp. 752-755.

"The Poet and the Nuclear Crisis," *English Poetry in Quebec*. Montreal: McGill-Queen's University Press, 1965, pp. 13-28.

"The Confessions of a Compulsive Anthologist," *Journal of Canadian Studies*, May, 1976, pp. 4-14.

# INTRODUCTION

This is a collection of essays on poets and poetry, but not limited like the essays in my former collection, *Towards a View of Canadian Letters*, published three or four years ago by the University of British Columbia Press, to Canadian poets and poetry. Two of the longest and possibly the most interesting of these papers, "The Refining Fire" and "The Poet and the Nuclear Crisis" are on much more general topics. The first, on the meaning and nature of poetry, appeared in the *Queen's Quarterly* in 1954 and soon after as a chapter in a book I wrote and compiled in collaboration with an old friend and former colleague at Michigan State, the American poet and critic, M. L. Rosenthal. The second was read at a poetry conference in Foster, Quebec, organized by John Glassco.

Some of these pieces were left out of the UBC collection because the book was as large as circumstances would permit and some because their subjects overlapped: none, however, because they were inferior or second-best. I think it useful to have the 1943 introduction to the first edition of *The Book of Canadian Poetry* available for comparison with later versions and with the long reviews by Northrop Frye and John Sutherland—one favorable and one very far from favorable. I am glad too to be able to reprint in a more or less permanent form the semi-autobiographical "Confessions of a Compulsive Anthologist" read last March at a conference at Trent University in honour of Professor Gordon Roper. In this essay I have omitted the final paragraph, which repeats the conclusion of the early essay on anthologies, and substituted a brief closing sentence.

The arrangement here, unlike that of *Towards a View*, is chronological, so perhaps I do not need to repeat the warning that the date of a critical essay or review needs always to be kept in mind. I do so anyway, as it is such a vitally important point. Another advantage of a chronological sequence is that it will make clear I have not essentially changed my overall view of the development of a genuine, if somewhat rapidly forced, tradition in English-Canadian poetry.

I still think a division exists between what in 1943 I called a "native" and a "cosmopolitan" tradition, as it does in American poetry also; but as Northrop Frye pointed out, it is a division not between groups or schools of poets but a division in the hearts and minds of every individual poet. I do not believe, however, that this division, which Margaret Atwood sees in Susanna Moodie as paranoid schizophrenia and calls Canada's mental illness, exists as a wound or sickness in the best poets of the astonishing revival of the sixties and the seventies. In Birney, Purdy, Avison, Phyllis Webb, Page, Layton, and Jones, to name but a few, an intellectual and an emotional force come together and strengthen one another. What I wrote towards the end of the 1943 Introduction is as true today as it was then—and more intensely apposite: "The older masters [Roberts, Carman, and Lampman] had sought a spiritual nourishment in the beauty of their natural surroundings. For them, the challenge of environment strengthened both the moral virtues and the aesthetic sensibilities and led ultimately to a powerful feeling of communion with the Divine Spirit, more or less pantheistically conceived. The poets of today, inheritors of what I. A. Richards called the "neutralisation of nature," have turned away from all this. They have sought in man's own mental and social world for a subject matter they can no longer find in the beauty of nature—a beauty that is either deceptive or irrelevant. . . . Generally speaking, it is the poetry of ideas, of social criticism, of wit and satire that has replaced the descriptive or contemplative poetry of the nineteenth century."

It is not that the new poets of the contemporary revival have reacted violently from the piety or the rather blatant nationalism that characterised our poetry almost to mid-century but, like poets in many other countries, they have increasingly found their material "in the world-wide revolutionary movement of modern times, in the new developments in psychology and anthropology, and in the elaborate techniques and abstruse theories of American and European writers . . . "

The only modification I think this passage written nearly thirty-five years ago needs to bring it up to date is to say that the "American and European writers" who were influential then were Eliot, Pound, Valery, Rilke, and Yeats, while today they are Williams, Olson, Lorca, Neruda, Brecht, and René Char—AND, it is good to be able to add, Frye, Pratt, Birney, and Layton.

Before ending this brief Introduction I would like to say that I hope nobody will be surprised to find three or four of these essays written in verse. A number of my poems, as George Woodcock and William Toye have pointed out, are actually criticism—pastiche, parody, burlesque, tribute, and translation. Indeed, the lines on F. R. Scott's birthday are better criticism, if only because more concise, than the formal essay in *Canadian Literature*, and it concludes with a passage in praise of socially and politically engaged poetry that may help to correct the view of my verse as nothing but a "difficult, lonely music," lofty and indifferent. The two book-reviews are lighter and are intended to be funny as well as perceptive. They should provide a change of tone, if nothing else.

A. J. M. Smith

# Canadian Anthologies, New and Old
## 1942

The publication, in Canada, the United States, and England, of a compact anthology of Canadian poetry in the widely circulated Penguin Books[1] is an event of more than literary importance. For quite apart from its merit the new book seems, as one of the reviewers in the Toronto press put it, "foredoomed" to have a big sale not only in Canada but throughout the whole English-speaking world. People in England and America who want to know whether Canada has an intellectual and spiritual identity are going to seek an answer in the hundred and twenty pages of this book. That they may perhaps be a little disappointed is not Mr. Gustafson's fault. His scope was hardly large enough, and he has wisely avoided attempting the impossible. There is refreshingly little in his introduction—as there is much in the prefaces of previous anthologists—about Nationhood, Empire, the Canadian Spirit, and abstractions of that sort. Instead he merely tells us that he has tried to make a small collection of good poems written by Canadians since Confederation. "I have measured and judged my material," he writes, "not by historical significance nor by 'Canadianism' but in terms of vitality. . . . I am hoping that the poems herein will become synonymous with *pleasure*." This is admirable, for it enables us to discuss the book as poetry and to discover why, although it is much slighter than many previous Canadian anthologies, it is one of the best that has ever been made. Such a statement is not in itself, alas, very high praise, and there is much more to be said in favour of the new collection than that, just as there is something to be said also about the weakening effect of the limitations imposed upon the compiler. The book is so good that we are surprised and a little annoyed that it isn't better.

It is the purpose of this article to examine the new anthology in the light of some of the more important anthologies which, from 1864 to the present, have given us a series of views of

---

[1] *Anthology of Canadian Poetry* (*English*), compiled by Ralph Gustafson, Penguin Books, 1942.

Canadian poetry at various stages of its development and have helped to establish a tradition of ideas and values that are now in the process of being modified under the impact of criticism like that of Mr E. K. Brown and Mr W. E. Collin, and poetry like that of the younger writers represented in the final pages of Mr Gustafson's collection.

One of the most surprising things about Canadian anthologies is the number of them. In addition to the inclusive major works —Edward Hartley Dewart's *Selections from Canadian Poets* (1864), W. D. Lighthall's *Songs of the Great Dominion* (1889), Theodore Harding Rand's *A Treasury of Canadian Verse* (1900), Wilfred Campbell's *Oxford Book of Canadian Verse* (1913), and John W. Garvin's *Canadian Poets* (1916 and 1926)—there have been a number of small fastidious selections of short lyrics—Mrs S. Frances Harrison's *A Canadian Birthday Book* (1887) and Lawrence J. Burpee's *Flowers from a Canadian Garden* (1909) and *A Century of Canadian Sonnets* (1910) are the best of these—and a fairly large number of books designed for use in schools and colleges. Among these one of the best was E. A. Hardy's *Selections from Canadian Poets* (1906), though the most useful to the student today is Carman and Pierce's *Our Canadian Literature* (revised 1935). A. M. Stephen's *Golden Treasury of Canadian Lyrics* (1928) is mainly maple fudge, while the explanatory notes are on an appropriately puerile level.

One of the most useful functions of an anthology is to introduce the work of young or unknown writers or to present new developments in technique and feeling. The last pages of the new collection concern themselves with this task, but there have been two significant little books, one published as early as 1893 and one as recently as 1936, which were mainly occupied with this pioneering work. These were J. E. Wetherell's *Later Canadian Poems* and a group production entitled *New Provinces*, which contained peoms by E. J. Pratt, Robert Finch, Leo Kennedy, A. M. Klein, F. R. Scott, and the present writer. Wetherell's book, apart from its small range, is one of the best of Canadian anthologies. It came at the beginning of a remarkable period in Canadian literature and was able to present excellent selections from the work of Carman, Lampman, Roberts, Duncan Campbell Scott, Campbell, and Frederick George Scott. It is one of the few anthologies that does justice to the poetry of George Frederick Cameron. *New Provinces* in comparison is a slight achievement. This, however, does not include that modern Canadian poetry is inferior (except perhaps in bulk) to that of the eighties and nineties. The slightness of the book is due partly

to the timidity of Canadian publishers and partly to the prejudice that most of the contributors felt against size and inflation,
whether of thought or feeling. They aimed at brevity, wit, and
intellectual concentration, and eschewed the ambition to be
major poets as surely as the contributors to Wetherell clung to it.
Two other anthologies of this type ought to be mentioned in
passing. They are Nathaniel Benson's *Modern Canadian Poetry*
(1930) and Ethel Hume Bennet's *New Harvesting* (1938). These
both performed useful work, though not so much as they might
have if they had not been so corrupted by gentility. This at least
was not the fault of Professor E. K. Brown's Canadian number
of *Poetry* (Chicago, April, 1941), which must be considered as a
small anthology of modern Canadian verse. What was most impressive about this issue was the general level of skill and intelligence in the verse and the thoroughness and brilliance of the
critical material that accompanied it.

These are not all the anthologies of Canadian poetry, but they
are the more signifcant ones. Most important of all, because
unfortunately they *are* Canadian poetry, or all that is known of it,
are the big general anthologies; and it is upon these that we must
concentrate.

## II

The first anthology of English-Canadian verse was published in
Montreal in 1864. Its complete title was *Selections from Canadian Poets, With Occasional Critical and Biographical Notes and
an Introductory Essay on Canadian Poetry*, by Edward Hartley
Deward, D.D. The compiler's intentions were sensible and modest. Dr Dewart comes closer than any other editor to Mr Gustafson's simple determination merely to present some good poems
by Canadians, and he makes the most of his rather poor material
by supplying a critical introduction that is still relevant at many
points to the situation today. The text consists of 172 poems by
47 authors, and the poems are divided into three groups, Sacred
and Reflective, Descriptive and National and Miscellaneous
Pieces, containing respectively 32, 59, and 81 poems. Within
each group the poems are arranged according to theme and
mood in the manner of Palgrave's *Golden Treasury*. The largest
space is given to Charles Sangster, the next to Alexander Mc-
Lachlan, the backwoods poet, and the next to Heavysege. Sangster is declared to be Canada's greatest poet.

Most of the poems in the book seem "elegant" and old-
fashioned. They might find a place in one of those handsomely

bound collections of album verses drawn from the popular ladies' magazines and found in Victorian drawing-rooms. Sentimental piety, melodramatic emotion, and conventional feeling about nature, expressed in rather dull verse, make up the greater part of the book. Yet this is what might have been expected, and to dismiss the book with a patronizing sneer would be extremely foolish. It had certain very positive virtues, and as a pioneer anthology, coming at the end of one period of Canadian literature and the beginning of another, it helped to clear the atmosphere and point the way to the future. It was prefaced by a serious and intelligent essay, and in the biographical and critical notes scattered throughout the text it presented a correct evaluation of the two or three leading poets of the time. And it contained a small number—perhaps twenty—of good sound poems that can still be read as poems, not as curiosities.

The most useful function of the book today, of course, is to supply the curious student of Canadian culture with a wealth of bibiliographical and critical information about the literature of the first half of the nineteenth century, while the introduction offers him an intelligent discussion of the problems faced by the Canadian poet-problems that do not seem to have been solved but to have been intensified by the development of the nation.

"There is probably no country in the world, making equal pretensions to intelligence and progress," wrote Dr Dewart, "where the claims of native literature are so little felt, and where every effort in poetry has been met with so much coldness and indifference, as in Canada." Even worse than popular neglect of "our most meritorious authors," he added, is the general absence of interest and faith in all nativist literature.

Only last year Professor E. K. Brown was writing in the Canadian number of *Poetry* sentences which may be placed beside those of Dr Dewart. "Even within the national borders," he observed, "the impact of Canadian literature has been relatively superficial. The almost feverish concern with its growth on the part of a small minority is no substitute for eager general sympathy or excitement. To one who takes careful account of the difficulties which have steadily beset its growth, its survival as something interesting and vital seems a miracle." Professor Brown analysed these difficulties with great perspicacity into their economic and psychological aspects: our subservience to English and American publishing houses, our colonial attitude of mind, our pioneer inheritance of a narrow practicality, and our regional loyalties. It is amazing to see in this modern appraisal the end-points of the various factors described by Dewart in 1864.

It is the colonial point of view that both the later critic and the earlier assail as responsible for most of our weakness. "Our colonial position," Dewart declared, "is not favourable to the growth of an indigenous literature," and he mentioned particularly the unfortunate effect of the Canadian's sentimental attachment to the Mother Country and his intellectual subservience to her. Among other influences antagonistic to the development of a national literature he noted religious intolerance and political bigotry. And he was already able to observe that "indiscriminate praise, by the press, of some writers, in which, whatever their merit, the dross was largely mixed with the pure ore," had tended to give these authors "false notions of their talent and achievement." This indeed has a familiar ring, and so have some of Dr Dewart's other observations. The booksellers, he found, who make large sales and surer profits on English and American works do not push a Canadian book in accordance with its merits—the expense and risk being generally the author's.

On the subject of nationalism and poetry, Dr Dewart spoke with conviction. He was an ardent advocate of Confederation. "A national literature," he believed, "is an essential element in the formation of national character. It is not merely the record of a country's mental progress: it is the expression of its intellectual life, the bond of national unity, and the guide of national energy." He doubted whether a people could be "united politically, without the subtle but powerful cement of patriotic literature," and expressed regret that the "tendency to sectionalism and disintegration, which is the political weakness of Canada, meets no counterpoise in the literature of the country." The persistence of that disintegrating sectionalism was noted by Professor Brown, and it is one of the factors which led him to the chastening conclusion that "Canadian literature has come into existence without any real impulse from the national life,"—a judgment which, if sound, indicates the withering of the high hopes that were to be so eloquently uttered by the critic and anthologist who, flushed with the enthusiasm of the eighties, presented us with the second important anthology of Canadian poetry.

### III

W. D. Lighthall's *Songs of the Great Dominion* was published in England in 1889, just a quarter of a century after Dewart's pioneer effort. The contrast between the two books is startling. The early work is a museum piece, useful, interesting, and quaint, showing only the first faint signs of a developing national literature; but in Lighthall we are in the familiar company of the poets, then in the first flush of their power, who have now taken their places as the classics of our golden age. Lighthall was well aware of the advance and was anxious to illustrate it clearly: "The most remarkable point of difference between the selections of Dewart and the poetry which has followed, is the tone of exultation and confidence which the singers have assumed since Confederation, for up to that epoch the verse was apologetic and depressed. Everything now points hopefully. Not only is the poetry more confident, but far better."

Confidence and enthusiasm pervade the whole of Lighthall's anthology. Nationalism and Imperialism, mutually strengthening one another, are seen as the underlying spirit of the new poetry, which is presented as the characteristic contribution of "Canada, Eldest Daughter of the Empire, the Empire's completest type."

In the period between these first two anthologies Canada as a unified nation had come into being. It was a young, strenuous self-conscious, growing nation, and when the poets that make up the bulk of Lighthall's book were writing it was almost impossible not to believe that energy, courage, industry, imagination, and shrewdness, left to themselves, must work out an immense and brilliant destiny. Self-reliance and self-help—Emerson and Samuel Smiles—blessed by the Everlasting Yea of a teeming continent, these seemed all that were needed to unlock the rich store of good things that lay ahead for sturdy Canadians. Mr. Lighthall's introduction was lyrical in its expression of this faith. "The poets whose songs fill this book," he began, "are voices cheerful with the consciousness of young might, public wealth, and heroism. . . . The tone of them is *courage*;—for to hunt, to fight, to hew out a farm, one must be a man! . . . Canadians are, for he most part, descendants of armies . . . and every generation of them has stood up to battle."

There follows a paragraph that is one of the most eloquent statements in all the pages of Canadian literature of that superabundant optimism and energy which hurled two parallel railways across the prairies and through the Rockies and sent Canadian troopers to die on the banks of the Nile. It is a remarkable piece of prose, suggesting here and there so very different a thing as Whitman's preface to *Leaves of Grass*.

> Canada, Eldest Daughter of the Empire, is the Empire's completest type! She is the full-grown of the family,—the one first to come of age and gone out into life as a nation; and she has in her young hands the solution of all those

questions which must interest every true Briton, proud and careful of the acquisitions of British discovery and conquest. She is Imperial in herself, we sons of her think, as the number, the extent, and the lavish natural wealth of her Provinces, eat not less than some empire of Europe, rises in our minds; as we picture her coasts and gulfs and kingdoms and islands, on the Atlantic on one side, and the Pacific on the other; her four-thousand-mile panorama of noble rivers, wild forests, ocean-like prairies; her towering snow-capped Rockies waking to the tints of sunrise in the west; in the east her hoary Laurentians, oldest of hills. She has by far the richest extent of fisheries, forests, wheatlands, and fur-regions in the world; some of the greatest public works; some of the loftiest mountain ranges, the vastest rivers, and healthiest and the most beautifully varied seasons. She has the best ten-elevenths of Niagara Falls, and the best half of the Inland Seas. She stands fifth among the nations in the tonnage of her commerical marine. Her population is about five million souls. Her Valley of the Saskatchewan alone, it has been scientifically computed, will support eight hundred millions. In losing the United States, Britain lost the *smaller* half of her American possessions: – the Colony of the Maple Leaf is about as large as Europe.

But what would material resources be without a corresponding greatness in man? . . . [2]

---

[2] A similar tone of exuberance appears also in S. Frances Harrison's *A Canadian Birthday Book* (1887). The work consists mainly of "elegant extracts," and for the most part seems closer in quality to Dewart than to Lighthall. It has some interesting bits from Sangster and Miss Crawford, and two or three little pieces by Bliss Carman, written especially for the book, that are among the poet's earliest published verses. Mrs Harrison's national enthusiasm is as warm as Mr Lighthall's. In some lines included in the anthology she undertakes to address the Motherland on behalf of Canada:

Yet, Mother England, that new land is fair. . . .
Her trees drop manna and her blossoms joy.
Her harvest never fail; her streets are full
Of her contented poor, her happy rich.

We might set over against these lines a poem of Alexander McLachlan that did *not* get into the anthologies:

We live in a rickety house
In a dirty dismal street,

This is poetry, of course, purer than most in the anthology itself, though these feelings find expression also in much of the verse that Lighthall included. Sangster's memorial ode on Brock is the only poem in Dewart that expresses anything of the power of this national enthusiasm, but in *Songs of the Great Dominion* there were many. Among them may be noted "Canada" and the "Confederation Ode" of Roberts, passages from Mair's "Tecumseh," and lines from Isabella Valancy Crawford's fine narrative of the frontier, "Malcolm's Katie," – one of the most powerful and intelligent expressions of nationalism in our literature.

The anthology contains 163 poems by 56 authors, and is divided into sections under the following descriptive heads: The Imperial Spirit, The New Nationality, The Indian, The Voyageur and Habitant, Settlement Life, Sports and Free Life, The Spirit of Canadian History, Places, and (the largest section of all) Seasons. These headings indicate the somewhat narrow emphasis of the book. Lighthall himself was well aware of its limitations. "The present," he wrote, "is by no means a perfect presentation of Canadian poetry from a purely literary point of view, on account of the limitation of treatment; for it is obvious that if only what illustrates the country and its life *in a distinctive way* be chosen, the subjective and unlocal literature must be necessarily passed over, entailing the omission of most of the poems whose merit lies in perfection of finish."

> Where the naked hide from day,
>     And thieves and drunkards meet.
>
> And pious folks, with their tracts,
>     When our dens they enter in,
> They point to our shirtless backs
>     As the fruits of beer and gin....
>
> And the Parson comes and prays—
>     He's very concerned 'bout our souls;
> But he never asks, in the coldest days,
>     How we may be off for coals.
>
> It will be long ere the poor
>     Will learn their grog to shun:
> While it's raiment, food and fire
>     And religion all in one....

This is the voice of "her contented poor," but the anthologists, if even for a moment they considered such sad stuff, took refuge in aesthetics (their standards were those of Palgrave and Tennyson) and rejected it as doggerel.

This is a limitation, it must be remarked, that much less consciously, and often more damagingly, has made itself felt in
some of the subsequent anthologies, which suffer not so much
because good poems on non-Canadian subjects have been omitted as because bad poems on Canadian subjects have been included. Lighthall's book is not unreasonably cluttered up with
fake Canadiana, and it is a real testimony to the compiler's taste
and literary accomplishment that it remains by and large the best
anthology until we come to Mr Gustafson's. Indeed, it is a necessary complement to Mr Gustafson's. Lighthall singled out the
new poets of his day for just and sensible praise, and he was the
last to do justice to the pre-Confederation poets. Sangster, Mc-
Lachlan, and Heavysege, as he was the first to recognize the genius of Isabella Valancy Crawford, and to hail the new poets of the
golden age.

## IV

In the first year of the new century there appeared an anthology
that aimed to free itself of the limitation of nationalism, so joy-
fully accepted by Lighthall. This was Theodore Harding Rand's
*A Treasury of Canadian Verse*. The opening words of the preface
announced that "the verse included in the volume does not treat
solely or chiefly of Canadian themes."

This seems like a real understanding of the truth that it is not
*Canadian* poetry we wish to find, but simply and all-sufficiently
*poetry*. Yet one is soon assailed by doubts. The anthologist outlines the dominant themes of Canadian poetry:

> Here are reflected the singular loveliness of our evanescent
> spring.... Every form of natural beauty is, in some degree,
> caught and expressed—sometimes in homely, sometimes in
> classical phrase.... A sane and wholesome spirit is charac-
> teristic of the verse.... The sympathetic reader will notice a
> marked pictorial use of nature ... as well as a sensuous de-
> light in nature itself.... He will notice also that nature is
> often humanized.... Nor are there altogether wanting in-
> stances of that insight and vision which beholds the phe-
> nomenal and cosmic with rapt wonder and awesome
> beauty-gleams, radiant symbols, or sublime manifestations
> of the immanent and loving One in whom all things con-
> sist.[3] ... Great personalities, high achievement, and noble
> character, also have inspired Canadian song.... A glowing

devotion to native land and a loyal and loving reverence for
our gracious Sovereign are characteristic notes. . . . Canadian
poets have given expression to Anglo-centric conceptions
and aspirations, diving with poetic insight the coming good.

One must in all fairness admit that this is more disturbing to us
that is was to Professor Rand's contemporaries. Yet it is not hard
to see why Rand will not succeeed as Lighthall had done. The
earlier anthologist had a buoyant, almost boyish, enthusiasm for
the robust phsyical life, and delighted in poems of action and
courage. Rand was a teacher and moralist, and though he makes
a point of telling us that he was "a Canadian by birth as were
my father and his father, my mother and her mother," he was
spiritually a schoolmasterly English gentleman. His book is academic and in rather frigid good taste.
    It is constructed on a much more ambitious scale than Light-
hall's, though its arrangement is the easy encyclopaedic one of
alphabetical order by authors. It contains 346 poems by 136
authors. Their merit is various. "At times he is an inspired
guide," writes Mr W. A. Deacon of Professor Rand, "and at
other times apparently lacking in discrimination." Indeed, the
majority of the poets included are forgotten, and though their
verse is for the most part respectable enough—quite as good as
that in the various year-books of the Canadian Authors' Association—it is mainly conventional and dull, the competent production of well-educated ladies and gentlemen who lack nothing but
an original impulse and an imaginative power of expression.
Scattered among these, of course, are selections from the genuine poets, which give the book whatever value it has.

V

A similar bias in favour of gentility and the Empire is found in
the next comprehensive anthology—the *Oxford Book of Canadian Verse*, edited, in 1913, by the poet Wilfred Campbell. From
the very beginning there was something unsatisfactory about the
book. J. D. Logan, who had himself a hand in trying to right
matters, described the preparation of the book in a brief chapter
on anthologies in his *Highways of Canadian Literature*. Campbell had been anxious to demonstrate two points: (i) that the

---

[3] Observe the tendency of Canadian anthologists to drop into
    pseudo-poetry in their prose introductions.

early poetry of Canada was worthy of more attention than it had been given since the rise of the school of '61 (in this he was right, though one would never think so from the examples he brought forward in his anthology); and (ii) that the Anglocentric Imperialist theme was of greater significance in Canadian poetry than the national. The manuscript disappointed the publishers, and it was revised by S. B. Gundy, of the Oxford Press, and J. D. Logan, who added some fifty poems from the work of current versifiers.

The book has rather troubled the critics, who have felt vaguely dissatisfied with it, but nevertheless respected the prestige of the series to which it belonged. Logan wrote:

> Campbell's Oxford Press anthology has been frequently appreciated as the best of the treasuries of Canadian poetry. But how a volume of such fortuitous origin and construction can be the best of the Canadian anthologies, passes understanding. As an anthology, *The Oxford Book* is more than any of the other anthologies of Canadian verse a volume of poetry "of unequal merit." But the defect most conspicuous in the book is psychological rather than artistic, spiritual rather than aesthetic. It contains 251 poems by 100 poets. It is the slightest of the three great anthologies[4] and the most classical. Its contents have dignity, taste, and correctness.

Whatever this may mean, the general impression it manages to convey, that Campbell's anthology is thoroughly disappointing, is true enough. But the trouble with the book is much more simply to be ascribed to is inclusion of a preponderance of dull and pompous trash which contaminates even the few genuine living poems that, it must be emphasized, are also there. And in fairness to Campbell it must also be stated that the poems added by Gundy and Logan (nos. 211 to the end) are almost a dead loss. Only two or three pieces by Francis Sherman are up to the level of the rest of the book.

In the introduction Campbell is mainly concerned to define what limits can be placed on the term "Canadian poet." It is significant that he concentrates on the first word, not the second. The narrowest definition is stated in the sentence: "Only he who has been closely associated with a country from early childhood, and has spent all the years of his youth and maturity within its borders, can fitly interpret its life and dramatize its problems."

[4] Rand's and Garvin's are the other two.

But Campbell announces another view, which, if less constricting in its Canadianism, is almost as much so in its Anglo-Saxonism. "After all," he writes, "the true British-Canadian verse, if it has any real root and lasting influence, must necessarily be but an offshoot of the great tree of British literature, as the American school also is, though less obviously.... What is purely Canadian in this offshoot of the parent stock must be decided, after all, by those canons which would constitute anything distinctly Canadian. But stronger even than the so-called Canadian spirit is the voice of the Vaster Britain, which finds its utterance in the works of her poets." Here, in this Imperialist traditionalism, is one of the anthology's basic weaknesses. It is the story of Rand over again.

Possibly, however, the final explanation lies in something even simpler than the editor's Anglocentric bias. It may be that he cannot tell the difference between good poetry and bad. In support of such a theory, I take a few passages almost, if not quite, at random from a collection which (be it remembered) is intended to be representative of the best.

From a hymn in praise of domestic felicity:

> A full content dwells in her face,
>    She's quite in love with life,
> And for a title, wears with grace
>    The sweet, old-fashioned "Wife";
> And so I say with pride untold,
>    And love beyond degree,
> This woman with the heart of gold
>    She just keeps house for me –
>
>                              For me, –
> She just keeps house for me.

From one of those red-blooded poems popular in the Jack London era.

> I was sired among the surges;
>    I was cubbed beside the foam;
> All my heart is in its verges,
>    And the sea wind is my home.

From a poem entitled "Innocence":

> Beneath her sloping neck
> Her bosom-gourds swelled chastely, white as spray,
>    Wind-tost – without a fleck –
> The air which heaved them was less pure than they.

And lastly, from a stirring riding song of the R.C.N.W.M.P.:

> Our mission is to plant the rule
>     Of Britian's freedom here,
>
> Restrain the lawless savage, and
>     Protect the pioneer;
> And 'tis a proud and daring trust
>     To hold these vast domains,
> With but three hundred mounted men,
>     The Riders of the Plains.

Where worse faults are avoided we have dullness and academic correctness. In place of the imaginative we have the fanciful; instead of wit, archness; and instead of power, gradiloquence. There are, as we have said, some good poems – Roberts' "Tantramar Revisited" and "Canada," Carman's "Low Tide on Grand Pré" (a standard anthology piece) and some of his Sappho lyrics, several fine things of Lampman and Duncan Campbell Scott, and a fair selection from Drummond – but once outside this group of "Classics" the editor is hopelessly at a loss. The selections from the early poets and from Isabella Valancy Crawford give the reader no idea of the peculiar merits of the poets before 1880, scarcely a hint that they possessed any at all.

What is particularly to be regretted about the *Oxford Book of Canadian Verse* is that the prestige of the series to which it belongs built up high hopes. Then, when the general hollowness of the book became evident, the reading public drew the not unreasonable, though quite false, conclusion that Canadian poetry is dull, correct, and imitative, that, indeed, to all intents and purposes there is no Canadian poetry capable of interesting an adult mind. Nothing could be farther from the truth.

A revision of the *Oxford Book* is badly needed. At the time of his death, Bliss Carman was as work on the task. The result would certainly have been a great improvement over the Campbell anthology; yet the transcendental bias of Carman's *Oxford Book of American Verse* permits one to doubt whether a Canadian anthology from his hand would have been really adequate.

## VI

Really adequate and perhaps a little more is what the collection that succeeded the *Oxford Book* was designed to be: John W. Garvin's *Canadian Poets*, published in 1916 and revised and enlarged ten years later, is not only the largest Canadian anthology—it contains 392 poems by 75 authors—but the most ambitious. It is the only one that makes any pretence of including a critical apparatus, though the apparatus included is nothing if not uncritical. The judgments on the poets are almost invariably favourable and they are inevitably capricious, for they are not, in most instances, those of the editor himself but are made by a large variety of persons whose authority, in a few cases of the highest, is in most non-existent. The selections from each poet are introduced first by a photograph, then by a "blurb" from a visiting critic, and finally by some biographical and bibliographical facts collected by the editor himself.

J. D. Logan praised the book in a characteristic paragraph:

> It is not only a repository of modern Canadian poetry but also a critical *vade mecum* to 20th Century Canadian poetry. For in addition to the poems in the volume, each poet's work is prefaced by a biographical sketch and by critical appreciation or comment by others than the compiler. The latter fact relieves the critical apparatus itself of the charge of personal bias on the part of the compiler. The Garvin anthology, again, is distinguished by a peculiarity of singular spirtual import. It contains nothing that is not *typical* of the Canadian national spirit and Canadian civilization and culture. Lighthall's volume, despite its good sense and genuinely aesthetic quality, had such variety and diversity of "notes" of the spirit in it that it is hard to distinguish which is the essential note, the typical voice, and which the "overtones" of the Canadian spirit. *The Oxford Book* again, is untypical of the Canadian spirit by way of too many poems that are "poet's poems"—too much of art for art's sake. But Garvin's *Canadian Poets* contains the work of such poets, both of the older and the younger generation, as expresses the typical work of each of the singers and the typical spirit of the Canadian people. It is a companionable volume; and it has the distinct advantage of biographical and critical comment, which fit it, according to its scope, for private reading and enjoyment and for critical study of the history of Canadian poetry. In those regards Garvin's *Canadian Poets* is an anthology which is at once aesthetically satisfying and pragmatically the most serviceable in the field that it covers.

Such nonsense has too often been allowed to pass for literary criticism in Canada. Any moderately skilful reader can see that

Garvin's anthology is *not* "distinguished by a peculiarity of sin-
gular spiritual import" – assuming that *that* means something. It
does not, for instance, possess anything like the spiritual unity of
Lighthall. It is diverse in theme and inspiration, and the quality
of the poets it presents is singularly uneven. One of its worst features is the responsibility-shifting critical apparatus that Logan so
much admires. The influence of Garvin's anthology more than
anything else is responsible for the outrageous over-estimate of
the "genius" of Canadian poets which passes for orthodox opinion in the meeting rooms of the C.A.A.[5]

If the most nearly contemporary material in the *Oxford Book* is
inferior to the rest, the same may be said of Garvin. Only Tom
MacInnes and Marjorie Pickthall were doing work of more than
the most limited interest. Pratt had not yet produced the bulk of
his characteristic poetry, and the younger poets, who enliven the
second half the Penguin anthology, were still just emerging from
college. Garvin cannot, therefore, be blamed for the absence of
these, but he can be censured for cluttering up the last third of
the book with a vast array of minor versifiers, whose stuff ranges
from the dull to the execrable, and from the pretentious to the
simpering.

[5] A few examples must here be collected. *Albert E. S. Smythe on
Wilson Macdonald*: "Who is Wilson MacDonald? Only the records
of palingenesis can reveal that secret, but I fancy that he has wandered from the lost Etruscan paradise and brought with him many
of the arts and mysteries that glorified that ancient people.... That
he is a genuis I have no doubt whatever. His many-sided nature is
outside the range of our ordinary garden varieties.... He has in-
vented new verse forms which compel the ear by their harmony
and the novel chime of the rhyme. He has shown that if he writes
free verse it is not for lack of facility in metrical art." *Agnes C. Laut
on Albert Durrant Watson*: "He sings because he must sing—because he has a great message to deliver, because he is one of the
torch-bearers to light the World-Soul passing through the dark that
ever precedes the dawn.... Something has entered Canadian literature with the sublimity of an Emerson or a Whitman." *Robert
Norwood on Charles Mair*. "As an interpreter of nature, Mair is at
one with Carman, Roberts, and Lampman.... In technique Carman, Roberts, and Lampman surpass him; but in strength of gesture
and firmness of touch on the great motives of human conduct he
outclasses them.... Charles Mair is not only the dean of Canadian
letters; he is our most authentic poet." It must be added that there
are a few critiques that are wholly admirable. Among these should
be named Dr Pelham Edgar's on Archibald Lampman and the late
Professor Cappon's on C. G. D. Roberts. All, of course, are short
extracts culled by Garvin from Critical articles and reviews.

## VII

It is where Garvin and the *Oxford Book* are weakest that the
new anthology is strongest—in the more nearly contemporary
material. This is not surprising, for it is since the publication of
the last edition of Garvin's *Canadian Poets* in 1926 that the
modern revival of poetry has made itself felt in Canada. Some of
its fruits are now, almost for the first time, being presented in Mr
Gustafson's collection.

The story of the book's publication is a curious one. It was
intended by the authorities concerned with the educational facil-
ities of the Canadian army to provide the soldiers with a small
pocket compendium of poetry in which the spirit of their homeland and the patriotic sentiments they were supposed to feel
might be found conveniently preserved. And Mr Gustafson was
entrusted with the task of compilation. He carried it out as a
young man and a poet might have been expected to. He did not
commit the error that one of our professional cherishers of the
poetic flame would certainly have made. He resisted (or he did
not feel) the temptation to fill the book with easy, commonplace
patriotic pieces and popular poetry of the maple-leaf school.[6]
Instead he has provided something that a Canadian may show
without mortification to an Englishman or an American who
asks, "But is there are Canadian poetry?"

The book is not, of course, a comprehensive and general work
of the magnitude of those we have been discussing. In a sense it
is an anthology of modern verse, and this is not only because
most of the exciting and interesting poems are in the later part of
the book but because the selections from the older, established
poets seem more perfunctory and conventional than they might
have been could the editor have brought to these writers the same
careful enthusiasm as to his contemporaries. It is regrettable, too,
that some of the minor figures were not ruthlessly sacrificed to
make room for a dozen poems of the pre-Confederation period—
a period that contains some poetry of an interest and a power at
present quite unsuspected. And, to get over the carping as
quickly as possible, it must be recorded that Mr Gustafson has
missed an opportunity to reveal the amazing quality of Isabella
Valancy Crawford and George Frederick Cameron. Pauline
Johnson is omitted, but the loss is not great.

The selections from the Carman-Lampman-Roberts-Scott
group are not exactly conventional; yet they do little to alter the

---

[6] He even leaned so far backward as to omit Robert W. Service
entirely, which is a pity, for "The Shooting of Dan McGrew" is a
vivid and entertaining poem.

impression that the most conventional choices would have given. The excellence of Lampman as a poet of landscape; Carman's masterly apprehension of the disturbing impingement of the mysterious upon reality; the superiority of Roberts's poems of the New Brunswick countryside to his more pretentious "cosmic utterances" or his recent patriotic verse; all this is clearly demonstrated by the selections from these poets. Only in the case of the poems by Duncan Campbell Scott must we note a failure to suggest the peculiar strength of a remarkable and underestimated poet.

Of the poets of the interim—the partially filled vacuum between Lampman and Pratt—the three most interesting figures, Francis Sherman, Marjorie Pickthall and Tom MacInnes, might have been more fully and more fortunately represented. One or two of Miss Pickthall's last Christina-Rossetti-like lyrics, "Resurgam" or "Quiet," would have shown her at a higher peak of achievement than the rather overweighted lines from "Palome." MacInnes is a charming and high-spirited poet who wrote an unforgettable poem called "Zalinka" that begins:

> Last night in a land of triangles
>     I lay in a cubicle where
> A girl in pyjamas and bangles
>     Slept with her hands in my hair.

It would have been a pleasant surprise to have found this in an anthology of Canadian verse. But though it is absent, there are plenty of pleasant surprises in the new book. Every reader will be grateful to Mr Gustafson for recovering from the files of the *Canadian Forum* the late Raymond Knister's deeply felt and objectively rendered farm poems. And here and there, particularly among the modern poems, but not there only, one comes upon discoveries that the older anthologies can rarely afford. Earle Birney's "Slug in Woods," Alan Creighton's "Spring Workman," Robert Finch's "Train Window," Neil Tracy's "I Doubt a Lovely Thing is Dead," W. W. E. Ross's "The Diver," Charles Bruce's "Words are Never Enough," Leo Kennedy's "Bitter Stream": these – and the list could be lengthened considerably – testify to the sublety, exactness, and intelligence of the modern movement in Canadian poetry. Among the older writers also we are shown some fine things that previous anthologists missed. Lampman's haunting "Midnight" and Helena Coleman's beautiful sonnet "As Day Begins to Wane" are found among classics no better but more familiar.

Another thing to be said in favour of the new anthology is that it is not solemn or stodgy. If for a moment it seems to sink, the book contains its own antidote and we can turn back for refreshment to "The Ahkoond of Swat." This is not the only example of light verse (why wasn't it in any of the other anthologies?), but it is perhaps the only piece of comic poetry, unless Mr F. R. Scott's "Tourist Time" which is certainly witty and satirical, is also comic. "The Wreck of the 'Julie Plante' " (which if only one piece of Drummond's is to be chosen is the inevitable right choice) is in part a comic poem, but it is something more – a genuine expression of the instinctive combining of humour and tragedy in the popular mind. We are grateful to Mr Gustafson too, for demonstrating by his inclusion of Mr L. A. Mackay's lines from "The Ill-Tempered Lover" that Canadian poets can express other emotions than noble ones.

It will be expected that the impact of the war should have made itself felt more powerfully than this anthology seems to indicate, but I am not sure whether the book is not more truly representative than a self-conscious anthology of war poetry like the unfortunate *Voices of Victory*. Canada has not yet come close enough to the smell of blood for it to enter the brains of her poets, and we can find here as yet little but vicarious emotion. The editor was wise not to include many war poems. Certainly the one or two examples of the work of the older poets in this vein are among the less fortunate pieces. It is instructive to compare the conventional "In Flanders Fields" with a present-day handling of a similar theme in Mr Gustafson's own "Dedication."

It will perhaps be fitting to bring this account of our anthologies to a penitential conclusion by confessing that I have been writing as if it were an easy task to compile an anthology and as if my own taste and my own opinions were as good, if not better, than the anthologists'. I have been complaining about their inclusions and lamenting their omissions, treating each as if I had expected him to be the ideal anthologist. What incredible folly!

The ideal anthologist is a paragon of tact and learning. In him an impeccable taste is combined with a completeness and accuracy of information that is colossal. To an understanding of historical development and social upheavals he adds a sensitiveness to the finest nuances of poetic feeling. He is unprejudiced, impersonal, humble, self-confident, catholic, fastidious, original, traditional, adventurous, sympathetic, and ruthless. He has no special axe to grind. He is afraid of mediocrity and the verses of his friends. He does not exist.

# Introduction
## to *The Book of Canadian Poetry*
### 1943

I

At a time when Canadian poetry is entering a period of renewed vitality it is good to look back over the span of a century and a half during which people living in Canada have tried to interpret the life around them through the medium of verse. It will help us to appreciate the poetry of the present if we can see it beside that of the past. Thus we shall come to understand the essential unity of spirit that animates good work in whatever age it is produced and in whatever style it is written.

The main purpose of this collection is to illustrate in the light of a contemporary and cosmopolitan literary consciousness the broad development of English-Canadian poetry from its beginnings at the end of the eighteenth century to its renewal of power in the revolutionary world of today. The emphasis, however, is not upon literary history or social background but on the poetry itself. Poetry is primarily an art, and it is most revealing when it is most itself. What it tells us about society is something we have to catch as an overtone from what it tells us about an individual. No extended effort, therefore, has been made to focus a direct beam upon the social, political, or economic background. Yet if the reader is not helped to understand that background a little more clearly by the indirect evidence afforded even by "pure" poetry, this book will have fallen short of complete success.

Whatever can be hoped for, however, the editor has been encouraged by the conviction, growing as the work progressed, that a catholic hospitality toward every period of Canadian literature and every type of poetry, traditional and experimental, ambitious and homely, does not demand the adoption of any ambiguous standard of excellence. The true standard, after all, is one of degree, not kind.

We shall, as Mr. W. H. Auden has reminded us, "do poetry a great disservice if we confine it only to the major experiences of life." In seeking to arrive at a just estimate of Canadian poetry we would do well to remember this dictum. Some of the best of the verse has been concerned with the homelier aspects of life, and its value often lies in a spirit of unpretentious sweetness that lasts well—sometimes long after much more imposing material has gone sour. William Henry Drummond's tender and humorous evocations of the olden times in French Canada are a classic instance of the preservative value of humility, humanity, and good sense.

It is when our poets have gathered their singing robes about them to hymn the mysteries of Life and the grandeurs of Empire that they have tended to become a little tiresome. There will be found here no prejudice in favor of "high seriousness." The significant tests are sincerity and vitality rather than loftiness of aim or solemnity of treatment. After we have made sure that we know what the poet is saying, we must ask: Does the poet mean what he says? Is his poem alive? We must impose, that is, a standard determined by the *pressure* under which experience has been realized, not by any preconception in favor of the kind of experience we are accustomed to label "poetic." Such an attitude makes it possible not only to take delight in the newer, and very accomplished, experimental poetry of today but—what is more difficult—at the same time to find pleasure in the verse of Canada's earliest period, which is sometimes vigorous, or curious, or even merely historically interesting, without being excellent as poetry.

Yet it is, in the long run, as excellent poetry that the greater part of the sequence of verses here presented must justify its claim to serious attention. In a sense this book is an act of faith. The compiler believes that here is an increasingly significant body of verse, at its best cogent, intense, and finely shaped, and that it may be presented as a not unworthy expression of the growth of Canada's self-awareness.

## II

Canadian poetry, indeed, is the record of life in Canada as it takes on significance when all the resources of sensibility, intelligence, and spirit are employed in experiencing it or in understanding it. Some of the poets have concentrated on what is individual and unique in Canadian life and others upon what it has in common with life everywhere. The one group has attempted to describe and interpret whatever is essentially and distinctively Canadian and thus come to terms with an environment that is only now ceasing to be colonial. The other, from the very beginning, has made a heroic effort to transcend colonialism by entering into the universal, civilizing culture of ideas.

To trace this twofold purpose back to the beginning of Canadian literature would involve an examination of the rather mediocre verse produced in the various British North American colonies in the last two or three decades of the eighteenth century and the first two or three of the nineteenth. What might be called the "extra-Canadian" tradition arose first. It could be illustrated in the hymns of Henry Alline and the rather angular poetry of Puritan piety, which was brought into Nova Scotia by schoolmasters, ministers, and judges educated at Harvard College. Under the impact of the Revolutionary War and the influx of the United Empire Loyalists, this poetry of religious ejaculation gave way to political satire leveled at republican "treason." The poets of the Loyalist tradition, of whom Jonathan Odell was perhaps the bitterest and the best, were disappointed Tories, who used the couplet of Pope and Churchill in a conventional and not very competent way. When they essayed the formal patriotic ode, the results were seldom happy.

Neither the Puritans nor the Tories seem to have found any compelling subject of poetry in the challenge of the new land to the sanguine and hardy settlers from Europe. But this was a subject that the Canadian poet could not avoid, though the lateness of its appearance is rather surprising. It testifies, perhaps, to the hardness of the conditions. The first poet who attempted such a subject on an ambitious scale was Oliver Goldsmith, grandnephew and namesake of the famous poet, who was born at Annapolis, Nova Scotia, in 1781. In 1825 he published *The Rising Village*, a kind of sequel to his granduncle's finest poem, and here, instead of the slow decay of a village of the Old World, he described the rise of a happy community of Loyalist settlers in the Acadian wilderness of the new. The poem has some touches of convincing realism and some instances of sincere feeling, but for the most part it is a rather conventional essay in late-eighteenth-century sentimentalism. The diction is familiar without being memorable, the heroic couplets are smooth and monotonous, and the native element is largely in the author's intention.

No poet of outstanding ability, indeed, was to appear until after the nineteenth century had reached the halfway mark. The task of subduing the wilderness absorbed all the energies of a young people. As the new century began, British North America consisted of a number of busy communities—Loyalist, French, and Scottish—in the Maritimes, Lower Canada, and Upper Can-

ada; but they had little to do with one another and, in the words
of Professor Baker, "nothing in common but a sense of isolation." It took events like the War of 1812 and the rebellions of
1837 to awaken a lively sense of the need for unity, and it was
not until the fifties and sixties that the national ideal began to
take shape in reality or to find expression in genuine poetry.
Then, if not in the old-fashioned, highspirited verses of Howe, in
the sincerely felt lyrics of Sangster and the descriptive poems of
Mair, Canadian poetry began little by little to individualize itself.

## III

The Honorable Joseph Howe was a busy man of affairs, proprie-
tor and editor of the most influential newspaper in Nova Scotia,
a politician and, indeed, a statesman, for many years the leader
of a sort of Nova Scotian nationalism that caused him to oppose
Confederation, though he was finally won round to its support.
As a poet he was an elegant amateur, whose descriptive couplets
and gaily tender lyrics were quite in the eighteenth-century manner. He wrote light verse, sophisticated and sentimental, and
sometimes, as in his own peculiar version of the Noble Savage,
the delightful "Song of the Micmac," at once ridiculous and
charming. The theme of his more serious work was the dangers
and ardors of life in the new land, and his most ambitious poem,
the unfinished "Acadia," represented an advance along the lines
that had been laid down by the younger Goldsmith, but no
important change. It is one of those long descriptive poems written in smooth couplets, filled with passages of moralizing and
relieved by anecdote and narrative, which were so much in fash-
ion in the eighteenth century. Yet the poem is not without interest, for Howe was closer to his subject than European sentimen-
talists. His diction and his moralizing are conventional, but he
paints the hardships, and indeed the terrors, of the settlers' life
with a moving honesty.

When Howe's "literary remains" were published in 1874, a
year after his death, they must have seemed like the product of a
century earlier, for by this time the Romantic movement had
long made itself felt. The Canadian poet who first came under
its spell and who attempted to breathe its spirit into his pictures
of the scene around him was Charles Sangster. Like Howe,
Sangster was to a great extent a literary poet, but the shades that
hang about him are not those of the eighteenth century. It is
Lord Byron, Tom Moore, Wordsworth, Poe, and the early Ten-

nyson that we sometimes feel through his poems, Sangster's two books, *The St. Lawrence and the Saguenay* (1856) and *Hesperus* (1860), have been long out of print, and he is remembered now only for a few pieces preserved in the standard anthologies. This is unfortunate, for the greater number of the selections do little more than tempt the unguarded reader to a casual glance and a patronizing smile. But to dismiss a man capable of the music of lines like

> "Love is swift as hawk or hind,
>     Chamois-like in fleetness,
> None are lost that love can find,"
>     Sang the maid, with sweetness.

or the gnomic strength of

> Ye whose souls are strong and firm,
> In whom love's electric germ
>
> Has been fanned into a flame
> At the mention of a name;
> Ye whose souls are still the same
> As when first the Victor came,
>
> Stinging every nerve to life,
> In the beatific strife,
>
> Till the man's divinest part
> Ruled triumphant in the heart,
> And, with shrinking, sudden start,
> The bleak old world stood apart,
>
> Periling the wild Ideal
> By the presence of the Real. . . .

is to dismiss a poet of unusual sensibility and of no mean power. Sangster has been praised as the first Canadian poet who made a successful attempt to express a personal reaction to experience in terms of his native landscape and his northern weather. Yet he is not exclusively, or even mainly, a "Canadian" poet. His finest lyrics are not his patriotic pieces, like the elegy on Brock (though this is not without considerable merit), or his descriptions of typical Canadian scenes, like "Chaudière Falls" or "The Rapid," but poems quite free from nationalism or provincialism, lyrics like "Mariline" or "An Autumn Change," in which a pure and elegant music rises out of thought and feeling and is expressed with a kind of stubborn self-taught solidity of language that is worth a good deal more than the fluidity and glibness of some of the more accomplished poets of a later generation.

Eight years after Sangster's second, and last, volume there appeared in Montreal the first book of a writer who sought to realize the poetic possibilities in purely Canadian themes. This was *Dreamland and Other Poems* (1868), by Charles Mair. Mair was himself to take an active part in the opening of the West and to make an adventurous escape from death at the hands of Louis Riel during the first Red River rebellion. The vast wilderness of prairie, the Indian hunter, and his prey—the rapidly vanishing bison—touched Mair's imagination, and in his most characteristic poems and his chronicle play, *Tecumseh* (1886), he tried to do justice to the drama of the white man's pushing westward amid all the romantic aspects of the Canadian wilds. Unfortunately, his verse suffers from the load of poetic diction carried over from his reading of the popular English and American poets—Byron, Tennyson, Poe, and Bryant—and it is very uneven in quality. One is astonished by lapses[1] that do, however, serve to throw into bold relief the lines and stanzas that are melodious and the images that are just. Indeed, although few of Mair's poems are satisfactory in their entirety, their best passages afford some delightfully precise close-ups of the Canadian woodlands and their flowers, animals, and insects, caught as they are under the parching sun of August or in the drenching moonlight of spring, and reveal in Mair an eye for the tiny realities of nature that many better poets might envy. Here and there, too, Mair shows a sensitiveness to strange states of feeling, which, in the best stanzas of "Dreamland" and a few other early poems, seems to promise an imaginative poetry that he was, perhaps wilfully, to turn away from. Yet if he could have gone on to write as sensitively and as powerfully as this:

> The silent shadows lay about the land,
> In aching solitude, as if they dreamed;
> And a low wind was ever close at hand,
> And, though no rain-drops fell, yet always seemed
> The rustle of the leaves like falling rain. . . .

[1] Such, for example, as the following quatrain preserved in Wilfred Campbell's *The Oxford Book of Canadian Verse* (Toronto, 1913):

> "Beneath her sloping neck
> Her bosom-gourds swelled chastely, white as spray,
>    Wind-tost—without a fleck—
> The air which heaved them was less pure than they."

he might—in spite of the lingering echoes of Tennyson—have deserved the eulogy his modern editor pronounced upon him.[2]

The greatest poet of the pre-Confederation period, however, has not received from succeeding generations of Canadians the high praise that once was accorded him by American and English men of letters into whose hands his astonishing dramatic poem *Saul* had come. Charles Heavysege came to Montreal from England in middle life and settled down to his trade of cabinetmaker and carpenter. A great reader of Shakespeare and the Bible, he took the themes of his ambitious poetry from the histories of the Jews or elaborated them in a world of Elizabethan sensibility. He made no effort to be a national poet or to describe the flora and fauna of his new home, and this, in part, accounts for the grudging recognition of his significance in the handbooks of Canadian literature. In these, the fact that he came to Canada late in life outweighs the fact that he settled there permanently and wrote his poems there. The universality of his themes is made a reproach that they are not "Canadian," and the originality of their conception and execution is remarked upon only to explain that he had little influence on the development of Canadian poetry. What appealed, however, to such admirers of *Saul* as Hawthorne, Emerson, Coventry Patmore, Longfellow, and Bayard Taylor was the richness and comprehensiveness of the intellectual and moral experience out of which the poem arose.

*Saul* was published in 1857, and in two subsequent editions (1859 and 1869) it was revised and improved. It is a mammoth drama, anticipating in form and machinery, as well perhaps as in its fine gloom, *The Dynasts* of Thomas Hardy. The play is in three parts, each of five acts, and altogether it is about ten thousand lines long. The third edition is a volume of over four hundred closely printed pages. *Saul* is a moral drama, conceived with psychological insight and with a richness of imagination that is expressed in a grandiloquent and sometimes grand rhetoric. What Heavysege lacked was not the ability to write moving and majestic lines but the power to construct an orderly narrative or a cumulatively intensifying drama. The play is episodic, and the spacings of its languid sections and its climaxes often seem haphazard. Yet the magnificence of the finest passages, such as the slaughter of the Amalekites and the ironic comments of the Demons conducting the souls of the slain to Hell, com-

---

[2] Robert Norwood, who wrote in his Introduction to the Radisson Society's edition of Mair's complete works (1926): "Charles Mair is our greatest Canadian poet by every count."

mands the highest admiration. So does the sensitiveness and power with which the King's madness is developed. In personifying the spirit of Saul's affliction as the vacillating agent of evil, the fallen angel Malzah, Heavysege has created a figure as orginal and convincing as an Ariel or a Caliban.

The other works of the author of *Saul* have not the scope and power of that poem, yet they are, in their way, remarkable enough. *Count Filippo, or The Unequal Marriage* (1860) is a brilliantly written and well-constructed problem play, very much in the manner of Beaumont and Fletcher. It analyzes with a good deal of subtety and a refreshing absence of squeamishness the moral risks involved in a marriage between youth and age. It is one of those rare things—a successful imitation of the Elizabethans—and, because of its poetry and its characterization, it is still good reading. A more conventional work and one which, despite its prolixity, has been more highly praised, is Heavysege's third and last major contribution to Candian literature, the blank-verse narrative, *Jephtha's Daughter* (1865). With it was published a selection of the strange and sombre "sonnets" that the poet had written earlier and that he now revised and carefully pruned. These reveal in little the strength and originality that make *Saul* a significant interpretation of the moral world.

## IV

None of these poets of Canada before Confederation had succeeded in creating a poetry that was clearly and definitely "Canadian" in the sense that it differed from the poetry of England as the flowers and foliage, the lakes and rivers, and the mountains and the very air itself of Canada differed from those of the mother-country. From the beginning it had been expected that a national poet would arise to celebrate the wild nobility of the scenery and to voice the aspirations of the colonists to become the citizens of a strong, united nation. Standish O'Grady, a disgruntled Irishman, who published in 1842 the first and only canto of *The Emigrant: A Poem, in Four Cantos*, was expressing a common thought when he wrote in the Preface:

> This expanded and noble continent will no doubt furnish fit matter for the Muse. The diversity of climate, the richness of soil, the endearing qualities of a genial atmosphere must no doubt furnish a just excitement to the poetic mind, and arouse that energy correspondent with a richness of scenery, which the contemplative mind will studiously portray....

Some twenty years later Dr. Henry J. Morgan, in his valuable *Sketches of Celebrated Canadians and Persons Connected with Canada* (1865), translated this thought into the present tense and applied it to "Mr. Sangster, the Poet":

> We in Canada are unfortunate enough not to have had many persons entitled to the distinction of being marked as poets, though possessing every facility that a grand and romantic scenic country presents, capable of exciting the proper inspiration and spirit of poetry.... The gentleman whose name heads this notice stands in the first rank of our Canadian poets.

The same implication, namely, that the whole duty of the poet in Canada is to be "Canadian," had already been made in the Introduction to our first anthology, the Reverend Edward Hartley Dewart's *Selections from Canadian Poets* (1864), and here also it was Sangster who had been designated first of Canadian poets:

> Indeed, in the variety of subjects selected from the scenery, seasons, and past history of this country and in the success and originality with which he has treated them, he has no competitor whatever. His genius is more truly Canadian than that of any other poet of distinction in this Province.

Sangster was not—though perhaps he wanted to be—a Canadian poet of this type. Dr. Dewart and Dr. Morgan were indulging in wishful thinking. The test is the quality of the poetry. Sangster's best work is literary, and it is English. The pretty passage included here from *The St. Lawrence and the Saguenay* has the quaint charm of a Bartlett print, and it is written throughout in the language of *The Lady of the Lake*. The village where Mariline dwells is the village of Tennyson's May Queen; but out of it, in the strange final section at least, Sangster creates his most impressive poetry.

Mair makes a more consistent effort to become a national poet; but, although he has excellent powers of observation, their expression is defeated by a ruminating and undistinguished mind. His treatment of nature—apart from the language—is still that of Thomson and Cowper. In contrast to Lampman and the romantic nature poets who were soon to arise, he is impersonal, conventional, and calm—accurate enough as an observer but not vivid enough as a writer. He is reflective and sentimental, not imaginative or intellectual.

But there was one poet, a predecessor of Roberts, Lampman,

and Carman—a young woman who died almost unrecognized at the age of thirty-seven—whose poetry had the exciting vitality that Mair's lacked. Vivid, energetic, imaginative, intellectual—these were the qualities of the best poems in a crudely bound paper-covered volume with the clumsy title *Old Spookses' Pass, Malcolm's Katie, and Other Poems* that Isabella Valancy Crawford published at her own expense – and at a dead loss – in 1884. Although the book was praised in a number of literary journals in England as well as in Canada and by such distinguished persons as the Marquis of Lorne and the Earl of Dufferin, it was not until a collected edition of her poems was published in 1905 that Miss Crawford's real stature came to be generally recognized in Canada. Some of her lyrics—she wrote copiously for the newspapers in order to live—are conventional and sentimental in the peculiarly awful manner of Victorian album verse. But where her imagination catches fire, as it does in her poems of the Canadian wilderness, she writes cleanly and vigorously, with a rushing sweep of energy and with a boldness of imagery unapproached in Canadian poetry until we come to the contemporary work of E. J. Pratt. In "Malcolm's Katie" and "The Canoe" the spirit of the northern woods under the impact of the changing seasons has passed into the imagery and rhythm of the verse. If there is a Canadian poetry that exists as something distinct from English poetry, this—and this almost alone—is it.

With the work of Isabella Valancy Crawford we must link that of George Frederick Cameron. Cameron, a brilliant student at Queen's University, sometime resident of Boston, later a newspaper editor in Kingston, died at the age of thirty-one and left behind him a body of poetry as individual and powerful in its very different way as that of Miss Crawford. A selection of his poems was published in 1887 under the accurate title *Lyrics on Freedom, Love, and Death.* Cameron was a classical scholar, an internationalist, and a cosmopolitan. Clarity, strength, and suavity are the distinguishing features of his style. We are told that he had read Virgil and Cicero in the original before his fourteenth year, and this discipline left its mark on his tightly packed, cleanly constructed stanzas.

One has little difficulty in setting the work of Cameron apart from the dominant tradition of Canadian verse as it was developing in the late eighties and nineties into a school of descriptive nature poetry. There is no effort to him to do justice to any aspect of national scenery. His themes are political, personal, and universal. They rise out of an intense love of justice and a hatred of tyranny, a passionate desire for the woman he loves, and an inescapable preoccupation with the idea of death. His command of form and of metrics is admirable, and he has the rare gift of taking a somewhat artificial style and infusing into it a tone that is energetic, convincing, and almost colloquial. There are literary echoes here and there—of Poe in the earlier poems and sometimes of Swinburne; and the influence of *Maud* can be felt in the background of the remarkable lyrical monodrama "Ysolte." Yet this is of little importance, for the literary influences are generally well assimilated. The individual quality of Cameron's best poetry is an energy that rises out of the clash of wit and intelligence with the forces of sense and passion. In a romantic age he maintained some of the classical virtues. Passionate yet resigned, and enthusiastic yet disillusioned, he was able, in the last month of his life, under the shadow of death, to write:

> For we shall rest; the brain that planned,
>     That thought or wrought or well or ill,
> At gaze like Joshua's moon shall stand,
>     Not working any work or will,
> While eye and lip and heart and hand
>     Shall all be still—shall all be still!

## V

In 1880 Charles G. D. Roberts published *Orion and Other Poems*, and a scholarly young undergraduate at Trinity College, Toronto, Archibald Lampman—ignorant as yet of the poetry of Isabella Valancy Crawford and George Frederick Cameron— hailed the book with a significant sense of liberation and pride. Wrote Lampman:

> Like most of the young fellows about me I had been under the depressing conviction that we were situated hopelessly on the outskirts of civilization, where no art and no literature could be, and that it was useless to expect that anything great could be done by any of our companions, still more useless to expect that we could do it ourselves. I sat up most of the night reading and re-reading *Orion* in a state of the wildest excitement. . . . It seemed to me a wonderful thing that such work could be done by a Canadian, by a young man, one of ourselves.

Lampman's own first volume, *Among the Millet*, appeared in 1888, and in 1893 came that of his friend and fellow civil servant, Duncan Campbell Scott. The same year, too brought Bliss

Carman's *Low Tide on Grand Pré*. Thus it was that the work of four friends, all born between 1860 and 1862, inaugurated a movement that produced in Canada a body of descriptive nature poetry which, though it was sometimes indebted in style or inspiration to Keats, Tennyson, Arnold, or Swinburne, was at its best sincere and original, the expression of genuine feeling and accurate observation. Moreover, these poets had a command of technique, surer and less spasmodic than that of their predecessors, which lifted them above the rank of mere imitators of the great Victorians.

Of the four, Lampman, though he died a comparatively young man at the very height of his powers, left the most completely satisfying body of work. His reputation has suffered a little both from the injudicious zeal of his admirers among the older critics, who have tried to present him as an important philosophical poet, which he was not, and from the disparagement of younger men, who have charged him with living in an ivory tower on the banks of the Ottawa, unmindful of the pulsing industrialization of Canadian life. But the truth is that the greatness of Lampman lies in the purity and sweetness of his response to nature and in his fine painter's eye for the details of landscape. Sensitive, and indeed passionate, observation upon which the artist has imposed the formal elegance of a strict but never inert control gives to poems like "Heat" or the magnificent sonnet, "Winter Evening," a peculiar authenticity much more significant in its vitality than any didactic element, philosophical or social, that was or that might have been injected into his work. There are, indeed, indications in his correspondence and in such poems as "Midnight" and "The City of the End of Things" that Lampman would not have been satisfied to remain a poet of pure nature. Yet it is as a poet of pure nature that he achieved his best and most characteristic work, and to have been anything but what he was by temperament would, one feels, have been to court failure. His best poems have a timeless and placeless significance which, paradoxically enough, rises out of their faithfulness to the local scene and to the specific experience. In them the woods and streams and the changing seasons of Lampman's beloved Ottawa Valley have been fixed forever in the life-giving permanence of art. The Canadian poet, he had once declared, "must depend solely upon himself and nature," and it is because he recognized so clearly his powers and his limitations that Lampman commands so high a measure of our respect and affection.

With Bliss Carman the case is somewhat different. Carman is probably the best known of all Canadian poets, and it is true that the peculiar magic of his finest poems can transport their willing victims into a strange realm of sensation and feeling where pleasure and pain are curiously confused. There is a heightened consciousness and a delightful shiver in lines like these:

> Outside, a yellow maple tree
> Shifting upon the silvery blue
> With small, innumerable sounds,
> Rustles to let the sunlight through.

> Come, for the night is cold,
>     The ghostly moonlight fills
> Hollow and rift and fold
>     Of the eerie Ardise hills!

> The windows of my room
>     Are dark with bitter frost,
> The stillness aches with doom
>     Of something loved and lost.

> Outside, the great blue star
>     Burns in the ghostland pale,
> Where giant Algebar
>     Holds on the endless trail.

But this intensity is diffused too thinly through the body of Carman's work, and sometimes it is produced by rather tawdry stimuli or by no definite ones at all. Even the much-praised "Low Tide on Grand Pré," after a magnificently resonant opening chord, fades out into a vague and imperfectly realized emotionalism. Too often Carman was the victim of his own glibness – a glibness of feeling as well as of language. He invited his soul in a spasm of perpetual vagrancy to travel hopefully toward a spiritual goal that was attractive mainly because it was unattainable. Thus he affords an excellent, if minor, example of Mr. Santayana's class of "Barbarian poets," the two most distinguished members of which are Browning and Whitman, both of whom were among Carman's particular heroes.

Carman thought of himself as reacting against the effeminate poets of the decandent nineties, and he sought in the school of Stevenson, Henley, and his friend Hovey to sing the praises of the strenuous life, the open road, and the call of the far horizon. At the same time he attempted to express a kind of national individuality in his imagery of maple, tamarack, and pine. But the inescapable impression is that Carman, like so many other red bloods of his generation, is in essence a *fin de siècle* aesthete turned out of the overstuffed boudoir into the almost equally overstuffed outdoors.[3]

Charles G. D. Roberts and Duncan Campbell Scott, the two survivors of the group, have produced a large body of work that stands somewhere between the lyrical fervor of Carman and the contemplative precision of Lampman. They wrote lyrics, descriptive idyls, and dramatic narratives that had for their setting the forests and rivers of the Maritimes and the Ottawa Valley and for their theme the emotional and spiritual enrichment that the earth of the new land grants to the sympathetic dweller in harmony with nature. Of the two, Roberts has been the more prolific and the more various. He has always been an extremely competent craftsman, but his inspiration has been the most genuine in his simpler, less ambitious pieces. He began, in the book that so pleased Lampman, with classical idyls imitative of Keats, and then, after producing an elaborate elegy on the poet Shelley, he turned to a delicate and objective nature poetry which presented a restrained and subtle interpretation of his native New Brunswick. Such graceful and sensitive poems as "The Solitary Woodsman" and "In the Barn-Yard's Southerly Corner" and some of the sonnets in *Songs of the Common Day* (1893) shine with a sober veracity that gives them a high place in the regional art of Canada. These are Roberts' best contribution to the national literature, and they have a value far greater than that of his more pretentious work, which includes nearly all, if not quite all, of his erotic poems and most of his rather facile transcendental pieces.[4] Roberts has always been an active and powerful

---

[3] Because of the romantic beauty of his best work and because of the impressive bulk of his publications, Carman has suffered by being overpraised more than any other Canadian poet, with the possible exception of Roberts. The wisest judgment on Carman is that of Mr. L. A. Mackay, who wrote in the *Canadian Forum* (February, 1933): "At times, at his best, to the very end of his work, he retains what I think is his genuinely personal note; a sort of shy, awkward, half-inarticulate adolescence, its quick fresh exuberance, the smooth-skinned, soft-fleshed delicacy, and the graceful charm of one of Donatello's youths.

"It is the great mass of inferior work that hurts his reputation. Someday, someone will make the right, judicious selection, and Carman will be rediscovered in his true place, as one of the most agreeable of the American minor poets."

[4] For an excellent analysis of the irresponsibility of these see Professor James Cappon's *Roberts and the Influences of His Time* (Toronto, 1905), one of the classics of Canadian literary criticism.

personality, and his variety of moods and unquestioned technical facility have enabled him to keep in the forward van of popular feeling. Upon the death of Bliss Carman he won wide recognition as the unofficial laureate of the Dominion.

Unlike Carman and Roberts, Duncan Campbell Scott has not received the full measure of admiration he deserves. This is regrettable, but it is not hard to understand. Like Lampman, Duncan Campbell Scott is a scholarly poet, a conscientious and unassuming artist. His talent is quieter than that of Carman or Roberts, yet he shows a deeper interest in human beings and in dramatic action, and he is more fastidious and accurate in feeling. If he does not rise to the heights that they occasionally attain, neither does he descend as they sometimes do to an obvious and swaggering lyricism. His interest in music and his refined and cultivated sensibility reveal themselves in many carefully wrought lyrics of love and nature. John Masefield has testified to the magical beauty of his long ballad "The Piper of Arll."

Dr. Scott's lifework as an administrator in the Department of Indian Affairs at Ottawa has provided him with the material for many remarkable poems of Indian life—from "The Halfbreed Girl," in his first volume of 1893, to the tragic masterpiece, "At Gull Lake: August, 1810," in the volume of later poems collected in 1936. As an interpreter of the Indian, Duncan Campbell Scott is deserving of more serious consideration than is the widely acclaimed poetess Pauline Johnson. But Miss Johnson had special advantages: she was a real Indian princess, a genuine half-breed girl.

Pauline Johnson, whose Indian name was "Tekahionwake," was born in 1862 on the Iroquois Reservation near Brantford, Ontario. Her father was a full-blooded Indian, chief of the Six Nations Confederacy, and her mother was an Englishwoman. The poetry of Miss Johnson was much admired in Canada, where the romantic fact of her Indian birth, played up by critics and journalists, was accepted as convincing proof that she spoke with the authentic voice of the red man. She had a vigorous personality and an excellent sense of the theater. Dressed in Indian costume, she read her verses with great effect to audiences in Canada, the United States, and England. Furthermore, she was enthusiastically praised by a fashionable London critic. Theodore Watts-Dunton, who had been attracted to her poems in W. D. Lighthall's *Songs of the Great Dominion* (1889), hailed Miss Johnson as the accredited spokesman "of the great primeval race now so rapidly vanishing" and later wrote a rhapsodic introduction to her collected poems, *Flint and Feather*, which was published soon after her death in 1913.

The claim that this volume contains genuine primitive poetry or that it speaks with the true voice of the North American Indian will hardly be made by responsible criticism. Pauline Johnson's early home was not a primitive one, and she was reared in cultured surroundings. Her education was literary. "She had read Scott, Longfellow, Byron, and Shakespeare," Professor Rhodenizer tells us, "before she was twelve years of age."[5] She must also have read Tennyson and Swinburne before she wrote her most characteristic lyrics. "Shadow Lake," "The Song My Paddle Sings," and "In the Shadows"—her best-known pieces—are decorous imitations of "Airy, Fairy Lillian" and "Sweet and Low." They have a graceful and easy-flowing cadence, which presents admirably vague impressions of pellucid waters and shadowy depths, but they are as empty of content as any devotee of pure poetry could wish. There is nothing primitive about them, nothing characteristic of the Indian or of Canada. They are minor Victorian escape poems, and their music is that of the waters of Putney and the gently flowing Cam. When Miss Johnson tried to portray more directly and more dramatically the feelings of the aborigines, she became, in such poems as "A Cry from an Indian Wife," "As Red Men Die," and "The Pilot of the Plains," theatrical and crude. The rhythm is heavy, the imagery conventional, and the language melodramatic and forced. Her best work is to be found not in her Indian poetry at all but in one or two pretty and very artificial little lyrics.

Two other poets of the same generation remain to be mentioned: One of them, Wilfred Campbell, was closely associated with the four friends whose work has already been discussed. The other, Archdeacon Frederick George Scott, of Quebec, stands somewhat apart.

Frederick George Scott is not, like the others, primarily a nature poet, nor is there much in his work of a national savor. He is frankly and unmistakably in the English tradition of Tennyson, Matthew Arnold, and Robert Bridges. In his best poems noble and sometimes profound thoughts have been expressed in simple, moving language in a style that is sometimes both elegant and strong. His themes are the universal ones—nature, love, hope, the transmutations of time, the mystery of death—but they are presented with a serenity and sureness that bear witness to the consistency and discipline of the poet's world view, which is

[5] V. B. Rhodenizer, *A Handbook of Canadian Literature* (Ottawa, 1930), p. 1966.

that of Anglican Christianity. In contrast to the dominant romantic school of Carman and Roberts, Scott's poetry seems calm, if not cold; but it is the expression of an orderly world view, not of adventurous gropings isnto the half-world of cosmic fancy. It is a measure of the poet's personality, not an exhibition of it.[6]

Wilfred Campbell perhaps had greater gifts than F. G. Scott, but he squandered them recklessly. Both in voluminousness and in loftiness of theme, Campbell's work testified to his seriousness of intention, but the solemnity of his self-dedication as a poet betrayed him into grandiosity and triviality. He lacked the ability to write well enough for long enough, and the large emotional abstractions he concerned himself with in his odelike celebrations of Mother England and Vaster Britain seem now rather threadbare and tawdry. The same is true, in the main, of his mordant philosophical poems and his crowded Tennysonian dramas. Occasionally, however, as in the remarkable "Lazarus," he produced a striking and original poem, though he was too careless of form and too generous with padding to do it often. His best work is his earliest, the descriptive poems that evoke the vast emptiness of the northern lake country, which were published in *Lake Lyrics* (1889).

Turning now from these poets as individuals, we must try to make some judgment of their accomplishment as a whole, particularly that of the four leaders—Roberts, Carman, Lampman, and D. C. Scott. Orthodox critical opinion in Canada holds that their poetry represents the most complete and satisfying body of work in the whole range of Canadian literature and is perhaps Canada's most significant artistic and spiritual achievement. These poets are the Parnassians, and the nineties, when their finest work was appearing, is Canada's "Golden Age." Undeniably, their prolific output was astonishing in a country as careless of culture as Canada was then. But more impressive than the generous bulk of their "collected works"—or the fact that many of their books bore the imprint of London or Boston—was the unmistakable polish, the genuine literary aura, and the high conception of the responsibilities and privileges of their craft which testified to the seriousness of their ambition. Amid the

[6] This judgment, it must be recorded, is to be reserved for the best of Archdeacon Scott's poetry—that in the *Collected Poems* of 1910. His patriotic verse, in which he has expressed the vigorous faith of a British imperialist, has enjoyed wide popularity in the Dominion and is not without its value in wartime, but it lacks the authority of his earlier scholarly poetry and his religious lyrics.

enthusiasm this flowering evoked, it seemed as if the patriotic hopes of Dr. Morgan and Dr. Dewart had been more than fulfilled, and that Canada, within a quarter of a century of Confederation, had produced not one national poet but four!

It was harder to realize that the concentration upon personal emotion and upon nature, while it made for an easier success, meant a serious narrowing of range and sometimes a thinning of substance. Delicate sensibility and often accurate feeling went along with a good deal of rather commonplace thinking and conventional moralizing. The supreme values were placed in whatever touched the heart and spirit in the beauty of nature.

The claim of this poetry to be truly national, adequately sustained in the field of scenery and climate, must, on the whole, be denied to a body of work which ignored on principle the coarse bustle of humanity in the hurly-burly business of the developing nation. It was an awareness of a lack of complete relevancy that led the most acute of our older critics, the late Professor James Cappon, of Queen's University, to observe that "perhaps our best Canadian poets have devoted themselves too much to an almost abstract form of nature poetry which has too little savour of the national life and the national sentiment about it and is more dependent on literary tradition than they seem to be aware of."[7]

But this is not the last word on these poets. It defines their limitations, but it does not state their value. This can be done briefly. In one respect their dependence upon literary tradition is not a defect, for it was more fundamental than any mere surface imitation. It arose out of a belief in the continuity of culture, and in their best work it was a preserving and civilizing force. They have, it is true, except in their second-rate work, no message and no philosophy; but, if their theme was narrow, it was an important one, and they presented it with great variety, charm, and precision. In general terms, it was nothing less than the impingement of nature in Canada upon the human spirit.

---

[7] *Op. cit.*, p. 84. Literary criticism in Canada, which is firmly rooted in romanticism, has not often presented this point of view. Mr. W. E. Collin, in a valuable essay on Lampman in *The White Savannahs* (Toronto, 1936), and Mr. L. A. Mackay, in several brilliant articles in the *Canadian Forum* during 1932 and 1933, have laid the groundwork for a modern approach. They were anticipated in some respects by Gordon Waldron, a disciple of Goldwyn Smith, who published in *Canadian Magazine* for December, 1896, a forceful attack on the school of Roberts as poets of mere scenery.

## VI

The powerful influence of Roberts, Carman, and Lampman was both an inspiration and a handicap for their successors for at least two generations. In the often moving though slighter work or Margery Pickthall, Francis Sherman, and, more recently, Audrey Alexandra Brown, the tradition of romantic nature poetry became brittle and glazed, and its imagery, which in the older poets had been genuinely local, tended to harden into convention. The Pre-Raphealite movement and the Celtic Twilight were influences from Europe that weakened rather than strengthened the poetry of the interim. To Margery Pickthall, the most gifted poet of her generation, they provided the framework of a dream world in which she created a graceful and nostalgic poetry, from which at the end of her life she wanted to escape into reality. And she succeeded, in some of her last lyrics in infusing an intense awareness of the beauty and transcience of life with the mystic's aboration of God. The beautiful "Resurgam" and the strange little poem "Quiet" are as striking in their ways as the finest lyrics of Christina Rossetti.

But the writer of this generation who came most strongly under the domination of the Pre-Raphealites was the New Brunswick poet Francis Sherman. An ardent admirer of William Morris and a follower of Carman, Sherman produced a small body of carefully wrought poems in the best of which nature is interpreted through feelings that become dramatic because of their intensity and mercurial responsiveness. But the colourful monotony of the background and what is intended to be a pregnant vagueness of the whole emotional situation imposes a richly decorated but opaque screen between the reader and reality.

A personality stronger than Miss Pickthall or Sherman—strong enough, indeed, if not to escape the prevailing romantic influences at least to find them in new forms and to transmit them in an original way—was the westerner, Tom MacInnes, whose "Rhymes of a Rounder" (1913) is one of the most engaging volumes in Canadian literature. MacInnes' originality consists in the gusto and skill with which he has used the Old French forms ballade, villanelle, and rondeau—for the expression of a genial and intelligent bohemianism.

At its base MacInnes' philosophy is as dark as Thomas Hardy's, but, like Dr. Johnson's friend Edwards, the poet finds "cheerfulness is always breaking in," and he is saved from the despair that is the natural goal of a thorough going materialism by an obstinate faith, the sources of which are human sympathy, sheer sensuous joy of living, and a feeling for artistic form. "God must be fascinated with matter," he wrote, with conscious ambiguity, "seeing he has made so much of it." MacInnes is a philosopher in the popular sense: he is concerned with the problem of how to live as well as we can under the limiting conditions of circumstances and natural depravity. "I mean well, but I mean to live," he remarks quietly, and he has found words for the inarticulate wisdom of countless millions. He is willing to accept life as an eternal struggle in which the joyous and the strong survive, and here he speaks with the composite voice of the generations of Jack London and Teddy Roosevelt. "We who are all in the mud together," he writes in a "Ballade of Virtues," "make too much of right and wrong: Three virtues sum it all— Courage, Cleanliness, Charity." He utters a curse against all meddlers—"ministers, medicals, meddlesome wives"—and finds a good word for one kind of meddling only, the helping hand to the down-and-out:

> Whether at sea or whether on shore,
>     Or at the job or over the wine,
> Whether on two legs, whether on four—
>     All good fellows are friends of mine.

The same salty honesty with which MacInnes celebrates the less heroic pleasures compels him to recognize the pain and cruelty at the heart of life, and in "The Tiger of Desire" he looks, with a Blake-like candor, at the truth that "fair and foul are close of kin."

Bohemianism, of course, had had its exponents in Canadian poetry before MacInnes. Carman and the American poet, Richard Hovey, had done well by it in their three series of *Songs from Vagabondia* (1894, 1896, 1901), mainly because they took it lightheartedly. But Roberts (and Carman in his later work) had been at some pains to dignify as a cosmic awareness or a spiritual responsiveness what was really only an ethical instability. MacInnes did not make this mistake; nor did another poet, a much more popular writer, whose sensibility was strong and crude and whose ideas were elementary. This was the poet of the Yukon, Robert W. Service.

Service has been read with delight by many who never read poetry. His work represents the lowest common denominator of the muscular dynamism, stemming from Nietzsche, that found various forms of expression in Kipling, Theodore Roosevelt, and Jack London. A strong, brutal realism, frankly melodramatic themes, and a heavy, clanging rhythm have attracted many readers, while repelling others. The ethics of existence are simplified into a justification of the strong, who, in the very nature of things, are bound to survive. But the harshness of this determinism is mitigated by a sentimental insistence upon a primitive code of honor. Much of his verse is trash, but in one or two robust ballads, of which the best is "The Shooting of Dan McGrew," Service has caught the spirit of folk poetry of low life—a poetry which blends violence, suffering, and high-spirited humor.

None of these poets who explored the varieties of individual romanticisms provides any link between the poets of the nineties and the younger experimentalists of the world between the wars. Such a link, because of the intensity, boldness, and variety of his work and because his sympathetic understanding is given to both the old and the new, is found in the narrative poet, E. J. Pratt. Indeed, it is from the publication in the *Canadian Forum* in 1925 of "The Cachalot," the first of Pratt's "little epics," that we must date the modern revival. Pratt, a Newfoundlander with salt and iron in his blood, has revealed himself as a poet of generous scope; and he is at his best when he has plenty of room, as he has in the fine series of heroic narratives, of which the latest is *Dunkirk* (1941).

Whether Pratt writes of the struggles of primordial monsters ("The Great Feud" [1926]) or of civilized man's battle with the elemental sea (*The Roosevelt and the Antinoe* [1930]; *The Titanic* [1935]), it is always courage and the lust for life that are at the centre of his theme. Though MacInnes and Service are both poets of the rough humors of the strenuous life and both are worshippers of strength and bravado, Pratt is a much more serious poet than they. In him, activity, however strong or brave, is not admired for its own sake. Heroic action is action directed toward an end and aimed at an ulterior good. Perhaps the outstanding feature of Pratt's career has been the consistency of his preoccupation with the heroic and the sureness of his development in the direction of reality and moral seriousness. This development has brought him in his most ambitious poem, *Brébeuf and His Brethren* (1940), not only closer to a significant moral theme but closer to a truly national one. Yet when he lets his muse out on holiday in a world of pure fantasy, as he did in *The Witches' Brew* (1925), he is unexcelled for high spirits and sheer boisterous fun.

Pratt is the greatest of contemporary Canadian poets, for he is the only one who has created boldly and on a large scale. His work is popular in the sense that it is never obscure, or even difficult, but it does not ignore or flout the intellect. In the richness and variety of his diction and in his willingness to experiment with new forms, Pratt points to the work of some of his younger contemporaries. But he has had little direct influence on them. Indeed, the very expansiveness of his good nature and the exuberance of his energy serve as something of a barrier, for the younger men are divided and complex, and, whatever virtues they possess, geniality and heartiness are not among them.

In place of the liberal humanitarianism that underlies the work of Pratt, they are more likely to find a congenial philosophy in communism, or humanism, or in the irony and despair of an aesthetic detachment. They feel that the tradition of romantic nature poetry which arose with Sangster and Mair and came to its finest flower in Isabella Valancy Crawford, Archibald Lampman, and Duncan Campbell Scott has finally played itself out. What, indeed, the poets of today are bringing back to Canadian verse is an intellectualism unknown since Heavysege and a merging of personality into a classicism of form that might find its exemplar in Cameron.

## VII

The modern revival began in the twenties with a simplification of technique. Following the lead of the "new poets" in the United States and the Georgians in England, Canadian poets turned against rhetoric, sought a sharper, more objective imagery, and limited themselves as far as possible to the language of everyday and the rhythms of speech. These reforms were largely the work of younger poets whose outlook was native rather than cosmopolitan and whose aims were those of realism. These poets sought to render with a new faithfulness much that had been passed over as "unpoetic" by previous generations. Some of the lyrics of Dorothy Livesay, the farm poems of Raymond Knister, Charles Bruce's stirring "Words Are Never Enough," the cadenced "laconics" of W. W. E. Ross, and Anne Marriott's fine example of proletarian poetry, *The Wind Our Enemy* (1939), are representative of this aspect of the modern movement.

But it was not in the simplification of style and the emphasis upon the harsher aspects of reality that the new poets made the most significant departure from the school of Roberts, Carman, and Lampman. The older masters had sought a spiritual nourishment in the beauty of their natural surroundings. For them, the challenge of environment strengthened both the moral vir-

tues and the aesthetic sensibilities and led ultimately to a powerful feeling of communion with the Divine Spirit, more or less
pantheistically conceived. The poets of today, inheritors of what
I. A. Richards has called the "neutralisation of nature," have
turned away from all this. They have sought in man's own mental and social world for a subject matter thay can no longer find
in the beauty of nature—a beauty that seems either deceptive or
irrelevant. Their early simplicity, assumed in reaction to the ov-
erloaded diction of much Victorian verse, has been replaced by a
variety of individual and subtle rhetorics ,derived in part from
Pound or Eliot, the later Yeats, or the seventeenth-century meta-
physicals. Generally speaking, it is the poetry of ideas, of social
criticism, of wit and satire, that has replaced the descriptive or
contemplative poetry of the nineteenth century.

The new poetry is rich and various; and, contrary to a good
deal of popular misconception, it is neither untraditional nor
formless. Most Canadians have yet to get used to verse that has
freed itself from the fetish of the exalted subject and the romantic cliché, so that when one of our younger poets[8] draw upon the
versification of a Jacobean dramatist to write a poem about a
salmon, the ulterior theme of which is man's economic rape of
nature, critic and anthologist are needed to testify to its value.

> Hung like a murderer with stretched-out neck,
> Prepared for dissection, absorption, use, . . .
> In gaunt symmetry lies the wonder fish;
> The trip from the egg to the waterfall,
> Leaping lively or lying sunned,
> The spawning, the schooling, the quick increase,
> Are value and profit and capital,
> No natural course is dissatisfied,
> No function corrupted, there is no waste.
> Use has been served up with vinegar, . . .
> All harmony, because all enmity
> Has logically come to stay; . . .
> For man and fish find purest pleasure
> In their prostituting mutual sight.

This is the language of the intelligence. The verse is traditional,
unassuming, and brilliant; the poetry rises out of the assimilative
powers of the mind and achieves its purpose by harmonizing
apparently incompatible features of reality. Allusiveness of imagery and directness of language are characteristic features of

---

[8] Ronald Hambleton.

metaphysical poetry, and they can be discerned in a fairly large number of poems in the later pages of this book. Kenneth Leslie's "The silver herring throbbed thick in my seine," Earle Birney's "Dusk on English Bay," Robert Finch's "The Sisters," Margaret Avison's "Neverness" and "The Butterfly," Ralph Gustafson's "Final Spring," Patrick Anderson's "Capital Square," and Patricia Page's "The Stenographers," with its vivid concluding image—

> In their eyes I have seen
> the pin-men of madness in marathon trim
> race round the track of the stadium pupil—

all testify to the success with which the younger Canadian poets have entered into the metaphysical tradition, which both in England and in the United States is now firmly established.

When to the qualities of the poets named we add the packed classical richness and penetrating satire of L. A. Mackay, the irony and social consciousness of F. R. Scott, the macabre lyricism of Leo Kennedy, and the passionate Jewish intellectualism of Abraham Klein, one begins to appreciate the variety and high level of accomplishment that distinguish the modern revival. The intelligence that this poetry reveals and the scope and power of the experiences it masters are the measure of a maturity reached before in Canadian poetry only by isolated masters—Heavysege, Crawford, Cameron, Duncan Campbell Scott, and Lampman.

Whether this new poetry is distinctively national is a question that our writers are not much concerned with. It is not that they have recoiled from the somewhat blatant nationalism of the 1900's into a disillusioned indifference but that they have grown interested in the world-wide revolutionary movement of modern times, in the new developments in psychology and anthropology, and in the elaborate techniques and abstruse theories of American and European writers unknown to Canadian philistinism. They are Canadian poets because they are importing something very much needed in their homeland. They are no longer in the exporting business, for maple sugar is a sickly and cloying commodity—especially in a world where, as a few recent war poems make clear, it is again possible to feel the tragic emotion and the sense of duty as a purifying and poetic force.

# Critics and Biographers
# A Review
## 1944

*On Canadian Poetry*. By E. K. BROWN. Toronto: Ryerson Press, 1943, Pp. x, 157.

*Sir Charles G. D. Roberts: A Biography*. By E. M. POMEROY. With an introduction by LORNE PIERCE. Toronto: Ryerson Press. 1943. Pp. xxvi, 371.

*Wilfred Campbell: A Study in Late Provincial Victorianism*. By CARL FREDERICK KLINCK. Toronto: Ryerson Press. 1942. Pp. xiii, 289.

*On Canadian Poetry* takes its place at once as a classic of Canadian literary criticism along with Cappon's *Roberts and the Influences of His Time* and Baker's *History of English-Canadian Literature to the Confederation*. The fine essays on Lampman and Pratt complement, and are themselves complemented by, those of W. E. Collin, while the study of Duncan Campbell Scott and the opening chapter, "The Problem of Canadian Literature," stand quite alone.

Professor Brown's brilliant first chapter makes it clear that the barriers placed in the way of the Canadian writer by his social, economic, and cultural environment are an intensification of the same ones described eighty years ago by E. H. Dewart in the first anthology of Canadian verse. These barriers are Canada's subservience to British and American publishing markets, her pioneer inheritance of a narrow practicality and a puritan reticence, her regional loyalties, and her colonial attitude of mind. With the growth of the nation they have grown more pronounced and more complex; and, thanks to scholar-critics like Professor Brown, Canadians are becoming more intelligently aware of them.

Indeed, the problem of the book is to account for the appearance in such unpropitious surroundings of poets as significant as Lampman, D. C. Scott, and Pratt. Professor Brown has given us a detailed study of the literary careers of the three representative masters and has related them to his central theme in a manner that gives the book a unity no collection of individual essays could achieve. The result is a credit to the poets and the critic, if not to the Canadian scene. What is emphasized is the isolation of the artist. Superiority, sincerity, craftsmanship, and a concern for fundamental values all seem to separate the Canadian poet from his neighbours and from an audience.

The author brings unusual gifts to his task of studying the Canadian literary scene. He is scholarly and intelligent; and he manages to be both disillusioned and enthusiastic. His standards are those of the humanist, and they prevent him from nursing impossible hopes. Furthermore, he has a sensitive understanding of the minutiae of poetic expression, and his patience in analysing the complex qualities of a text lends conviction to his generalizations.

In a book of this scope—small in size but wide and deep in its implications—it would be strange if there were no judgments to be questioned. I cannot help feeling that if Professor Brown had brought the same sympathetic insight he has concentrated upon his three major figures to bear also on George Frederick Cameron he might have discovered signs of the individuality he complains of missing. And I could wish that so alert a critic had not lent his support to the legend that our best poetry starts with Roberts. Such objections, however, are of little importance when measured against Professor Brown's bold affirmation of the truth that the romantic poets of the Roberts-Carman-Lampman school have little claim to be considered national poets. Of Bliss Carman's middle years in the United States he writes that the poet "did not become an American writer, but merely a *déraciné*, a nomad in his imaginary and not very rich kingdom of Vagabondia." And of the three leaders the critic remarks: "They usually write of Canada—and this appears in their images and rhythms as well as in their substance—as if it were a large English county, and it is hard for them to convey in their nature-verse any feeling which has not been more powerfully presented by one or another of the English poets." This is an opinion that the younger poets and critics of Montreal and Toronto will greet with enthusiasm, though one must not forget that no less an authority than the late Professor Cappon said the same thing in his first book on Roberts. The directness of these statements is something of a departure from Professor Brown's usual urbane caution. I feel that his criticism is most effective when his fine sensibility and enlightened point of view are given the most vigorous expression. Urbanity, polish, and qualification sometimes blunt the effect. The suspended judgment and the disarming acknowledgment suggest the Paris of Sainte-Beuve or the Oxford of Matthew Arnold; but our critic must be heard in the

Toronto of William Arthur Deacon and the Montreal of S. Morgan Powell.

It is for that world that Miss Elsie Pomeroy's life of Sir Charles G. D. Roberts seems principally intended. The facts of Roberts's literary success story are presented in rapid outline in a work which, though it has the bulky appearance and the idolatrous deference of an official biography, is closer now to the discursive small talk of the memoir and now to the matter-of-factness of the encyclopaedia. Yet somehow the book does convey the impression of a remarkable personality. Roberts is presented as a singularly gifted man, hard-working, hard-playing, enthusiastic, self-confident, with a genius for good fellowship and a craftsman's devotion to his art. He was fortunate in having many relatives and friends who were his enthusiastic encouragers. Like his cousin Bliss Carman, he moved in an atmosphere of delighted appreciation, not the least delightful being his own energizing sense of self-dedication as a poet.

Roberts' best poetry is his simple and beautiful evocation of the Acadian landscape. Most interesting to the historian, however, are the political pieces, few in number but significant in content. The poet's "political adjustment" is the subject of one of Miss Pomeroy's early chapters. In part, this appears to have been the result of a strong reaction against the annexation proposals of Goldwin Smith, for whom Roberts worked for a few months in 1883-4 as literary editor of *The Week*. "Roberts, in his fierce antagonism towards annexation, became, though for a very brief period, an ardent independent." Later he came "to accept most emphatically the fundamental idea of Imperial Federation," but he could not agree with Sir George Parkin's theory of a federal imperial government. "In future years Roberts condensed his view on this subject into one significant sentence; i.e., 'A good Canadian Nationalist *must* be a good British Imperialist'." Miss Pomeroy is content with a somewhat meagre survey of this development, but many of her anecdotes reveal more than her comments. Nothing, for example, could show more significantly the part played by Canada's great commercial enterprises in offering patronage both to the arts and to patriotic sentiment itself than her account of the writing of Roberts' Ode for Canada's Diamond Jubilee in 1926.

He, who over forty years before had written "An Ode for the Canadian Confederacy," was expected to celebrate the occasion in another Ode. His friends from the Atlantic to the Pacific, at first, gently, and then quite firmly, reminded him of his duty in this regard. The Government of his own

Province, New Brunswick, told him early in the year, that according to their plans for the celebration, he would be present and read the Ode which he would write for the Diamond Jubilee. It was a period of personal anxiety and temporary ill health for the poet, and the event seemed far-off. At first he insisted that he could not write it. But as the anniversary drew nearer, the impulse to create began to stir. Then Mr. Ivor Lewis of The T. Eaton Co. approached him with an offer to purchase first publishing rights of the new poem for a handsome sum. This proved an effective stimulus.... According to the arrangement made with The T. Eaton Co., the poem, occupying a whole newspaper page, appeared on July first in all Canadian papers in which The T. Eaton Co. were accustomed to advertise.

If Miss Pomeroy occasionally says too much, she more often errs on the side of reticence. Discretion is not a major virtue of a biographer. At times we are reminded of the scene in Virginia Woolf's *Orlando* where the hero-heroine meets Mr. Alexander Pope. "Then the little gentleman said, He said next. He said finally." Charlie Roberts met the great, too. But what did they say to him? Swinburne said (not to him, indeed, but in his presence, to Watts-Dunton—Roberts had called at No. 2, The Pines), "Walter, don't you think I might have another bottle of beer?" Matthew Arnold, who is described as "tall, not unlike Dr. Pelham Edgar in appearance," though he wore side-burns, said when he met the young Canadian poet at Goldwin Smith's, " 'This is the boy I wanted to meet,' and kept Roberts beside him." But that is all we are told of the conversation. Surely Roberts couldn't have forgotten everything that was said. And there was the meeting with Oscar Wilde. The English aesthete, in the proper velveteens and knee breeches, had lectured to a large audience in the Fredericton City Hall, and Roberts went back with him after the performance to his suite at the Queen Hotel. "Both being young and both being devoted students of the classics, they first poured out a libation to the Gods of Greece and Rome—a libation of gin in default of a more classical beverage. Then they settled themselves to the more serious business of the session, which was reading aloud alternately each other's poems with appropriate and eulogistic comments. It was a distinctly 'ambrosial night'." We would have liked to hear more of this encounter and might well have been spared in return many passages such as those telling of two visits to Halifax in 1939. "Staying at the Lord Nelson Hotel on both occasions he was able to visit daily his little feathered friends, the pigeons who live amid the hibiscus, poinsettia, and other tropical plants which flourish in the beautiful Public Gardens . . . "

Compared with Miss Pomeroy's book, Dr. Carl Frederick Klinck's biography of Wilfred Campbell is less lively but more scholarly. It is subtitled *A Study in Late Provincial Victorianism*, and the phrase aptly characterizes the peculiar brand of Tory Ontario imperialism that formed the heart of the poet's public philosophy. "The unity of Campbell's teaching," Professor Klinck writes, "—in all its various branches, transcendental, anthropological, ethical, literary, Tory, Imperialistic—is found in a common source for his examples and illustrations, the heritage of the British race." Campbell's attitude toward the United States is described as "typically Tory." "He had no faith in republican institutions; but he was Tory enough to expect the Americans to work toward 'constructive democracy'," and "he had hopes of a revival of 'race-piety' across the border."

It is hard to believe that such fatuous sentiments should have commanded serious attention. Campbell's imperialism was based on the theory of Anglo-Saxon race superiority, mingled with strains of Hebraic theology, Victorian complacency, and a truculent ancestral pride. The book traces with careful clarity the sources and the development of this philosophy and throws an interesting light on the poet's relations with the vice-regal ménage during the terms of the Marquis of Lorne and of Earl Grey. Later Campbell visited England and Scotland and moved freely in the society of the Marquis of Lorne, by then Duke of Argyle and the symbolic head of the Clan Campbell. What Professor Klinck refers to as the Duke's "gift of humour" and "rare sense of proportion" are illustrated by a letter Argyle wrote the poet in 1910:

> To one Radical friend of mine, I have just been pointing out a fact I discovered to my sorrow, that when one duly considers the constitution of the word Radical he has adopted as his title—that if one leaves out altogether from the title Radical the letters C A D, there still remain, unfortunately the letters L I A R. Curious, isn't it—and sad!

The value of this study of Campbell is that it contains things like this; its weakness is that, in spite of its scholarly documentation and the rewarding research that has gone into it, the author should feel the need to excuse a philosophy that is shoddy and puerile and to praise a poetry—the early nature lyrics excepted—that is inflated and flatulent.

# The Poetry of Duncan Campbell Scott
## 1948

The death of Duncan Campbell Scott has removed the last surviving member of the remarkable group of poets born in the sixties of the last century whose work, which began to appear in the nineties, established a national school of reflective nature poetry and achieved a standard of formal excellence unattained in Canada before and rarely equalled since. It is no doubt true that the spirit of rather blatant national sentiment, which was characteristic of our political and economic life in the quarter century after 1890, was operating in other fields as well, and it was responsible for these poets' being overpraised or at least being praised in terms that transcended and hence failed to perceive correctly their special and limited goodness. The times seemed to call for prophecy; and a kind of transcendental national optimism, instead of being allowed to flourish in the heady atmosphere of political oratory, was sought for (and rather too easily found) in the songs of the poets. Already a generation before Confederation, there had been a feverish effort to cultivate the national spirit in poetry, but such forerunners as Sangster and Mair had lacked the virtuosity and the scholarly equipment of the later group. It was Charles G. D. Roberts directly and Bliss Carmen, Wilfred Campbell, and Archibald Lampman more implicitly, and each in his own individual way, who demonstrated for the benefit of those who wished to see Confederation cemented by the rise of a national literature that the poets at least were willing to try.

The criticism that, at any rate in Canada, has focused its attention on these poets as the prophets of nationalism has made two serious errors: it has mistaken for national what is local or universal, and it has overemphasized the value of what it has chosen to see as national. Among the older critics, only Professor Cappon, in his *Roberts and the Influences of His Time*, seems to have shown an awareness of the fact that to approach these authors as if they formed a national school was to generalize about them and to miss the point of their individual quality. Recently it has become easier to see the poets of our "Golden

Age" in better perspective and to evaluate them in more significant terms. The work of such critics as W. E. Collin, Professor E.
K. Brown, and, more recently, Ralph Gustafson has helped us to
realize that we must first estimate these poets by the faithfulness
and intensity of their perceptions of the precise and *local* image
and then judge them as the nature of their poetry makes clear
they demand to be judged—in terms of the universal civilizing
culture of ideas. They take their place, it must be realized, in the
main stream of nineteenth century English poetry, whether written in England or North America, a current outside of which
perhaps only Hopkins and Whitman are clearly seen to stand.

Duncan Campbell Scott, whose memory I wish to honor by
devoting this essay to an examination of his poetry and criticism,
has been spared the excessive adulation that, directed towards
the wrong things in Carman and Roberts, has done their reputa-
tions a real disservice. Some of the reasons for the comparative
neglect of Scott's poetry are no doubt to be found in the special
kind of excellence the poet placed before himself as a conscious
aim. These are the classical virtues of restraint and precision,
and along with them also are the courtly and now somewhat
oldfashioned virtues of the cultivated gentleman, carried over
into the realm of sensibility and art. In a sense, Duncan Campbell Scott's poetry has been saved from the wrong kind of praise
by a sort of calm and isolated superiority, which has assured for
it also a reception that can be described as respectful silence.
Only Professor Brown has spoken out in behalf of the too long
neglected poet.

I do not think, however, that the whole story of the slowness
of the response to the poetry of Duncan Campbell Scott is told
when we have taken into account the calm, scholarly, polished
quality of his verse, which in its very nature is calculated to
appeal to the reflective and knowledgeable few. It is true that
Scott tends towards a precise and unruffled sobriety of expression, which makes it hard for those who are easily stimulated by
the flamboyant and the sensational to respond to work that is
generally so much less immediately exciting than Carman's or
Roberts'. Scott, in a way, must be regarded as a scholar poet, a
calm and contemplative writer, whose true exemplar is Matthew
Arnold or Robert Bridges, not Keats or the Pre-Raphaelities,
though, like the other Canadian poets of his generation, he
shows in his earliest poems influences of the most romantic sort.
But what sets him apart from his friends and contemporaries—
and even from the closest of all to him. Lampman—is the fact
that he made so little conscious effort to be a national poet, and

the Canadian element in his work, which developed as his art matured, has grown silently and apparently almost without volition, into the very unstressed essence of the work. This has meant that Scott was to be of little use to those who were anxious to prove the existence of a political or economic national unity by pointing to the expression of a national spirit in our poetry and our art. It is this absence of an obvious and easily demonstrated Canadianism that is responsible for the comparative lack of attention Scott's poetry has received.

All of this, however, makes it easier for us today to see Scott and his contemporaries in the right perspective. With him we have not to clear away the clutter of irresponsible adulation that has grown up around Roberts and Carman. In his case, too, it is possible to discern the kind of approach that ought to have been made long ago—to him and to the other poets of the group as well. There is no particular credit in seeing this now; yet it may be helpful to put down a few elementary principles that should guide our judgment of these poets and that should help us from falling into the opposite error from uncritical adulation—the error of too complacent and hypercritical an analysis that finds fault with these poets for expressing the *zeitgeist* of their time. To attack Scott, for instance, because he does not write like Stephen Spender is to be more ridiculous, if that were possible, than the panegyrists among the older critics.

What, then, should be our approach to the poets of the Group of the Sixties, and to the last of them, Duncan Campbell Scott? Well, in the first place we must recognize that these poets brought to the practice of their art a culture and a technical accomplishment that was based on deep and sound scholarship, constant reading of the Greek and Latin classics, and an enthusiastic study of the nineteenth century romantic poets and of the exciting contemporaries, the Pre-Raphaelites and the poets of the nineties. They were, in other words, more deeply versed in the essential poetic scholarship of their time, and, technically, as far as the actual handling of language is concerned, they were superior to all but one or two of our modern poets.

II

Duncan Campbell Scott's first book of poems, *The Magic House and Other Poems*, was published in London and Ottawa in 1893. In that year also appeared Bliss Carman's first collection, *Low Tide on Grand Pré*, Archibald Lampman's second book, *Lyrics of Earth*, and Charles G. D. Roberts's third, *Songs of the Common Day*. A poetic flowering was clearly under way. The first thing that strikes one about all these books is their responsiveness to literary tradition. They are the work of responsible and careful craftsmen who found in the landscapes around them and in the emotions of their own hearts material that did not separate them from the main stream of the poetry of England and of New England. Of Scott, in his first book at least, this is particularly true. *The Magic House* is clearly the work of a sensitive and refined student of poetry and of an exact and observant lover of nature. It is very eclectic, and one can detect essays in the manner of the Pre-Raphaelites, or the Decadents, or Wordsworth or Arnold. Sometimes a scene is painted in a way that recalls Lampman. But everywhere, too, are indications of an individual sensibility, a personal quality that reveals itself as unmistakably and quietly as the expression of one's face—and which is so hard to describe. It shows itself in Scott's early poetry as a faint flush, a strange half feverish glow that lights up the verse and gives it a curious tremulous exciting quality in sharp contrast to the "correctness" of the verse form. This quality is given the fullest play later in the long romantic ballad "The Piper of Arll," which has been justly admired as one of the finest of Scott's poems, but it is present, sometimes only in fitful flashes but sometimes more constantly in many of the lyrics in *The Magic House*. Here, to illustrate what I mean, are a few lines from "A Night in June":

> There is no stir of air at all,
>> Only at times an inward breeze
>> Turns back a pale leaf in the trees.
>
> Here the syringa's rich perfume
>> Covers the tulips red retreat,
>> A burning pool of scent and heat.
>
> The pallid lightning wavers dim
>> Between the trees, then deep and dense
>> The darkness settles more intense.
>
> A hawk lies panting in the grass
>> Or plunges upward through the air,
>> The lightning shows him whirling there . . .

And here is a stanza from "A Summer Storm:"

> The beetles clattered at the blind,
>> The hawks fell twanging from the sky.
> The west unrolled a feathery wind,
>> And the night fell sullenly.

These few verses are enough to illustrate Scott's early mastery of expression and the characteristic tremor of restrained excitement, which is one aspect of his most striking poems. This is a quality that Carman possesses more intensely and that shows itself more often in the poet of the Maritimes, but it is combined in Scott with a precision and clarity, an exactness of depiction that challenges comparison with Lampman. Some of the poems in *The Magic House*, indeed, have a Wordsworthian simplicity and a sober veracity that show the young poet could submit to influences that restrain, as well as to those that kindle. If he had caught some of the feverish glow of the Pre-Raphaelites and the poets of the Nineties he could learn also from the classic calm of Arnold and Birdges, and beside the lines quoted we can place others of a different sort, as, for instance, these from "Off Rivière du Loup"

> O ship incoming from the sea
> > With all your cloudy tower of sail,
> Dashing the water to the lee,
> > And leaning grandly to the gale . . .
>
> You know the joy of coming home,
> > After long leagues to France or Spain;
> You feel the clear Canadian foam
> > And the gulf water heave again . . .
>
> At evening off some reedy bay
> > You will swing slowly on your chain,
> And catch the scent of dewy hay
> > Soft blowing from the pleasant plain.

The twofold strain, one tremulous and a little feverish, the other calm, precise, and restrained, runs through all of the poetry of Duncan Campbell Scott. The best of the poems of the first type are "The Piper of Arll," "The Sleeper," "Night Burial in the Forest," and "Spring on Mattagami." Three of these are well known, though I don't know that anyone has commented on the curious effect that Scott has achieved in "Spring on Mattagami" by bringing into the Canadian wilderness an impassioned rhapsody rhythmically and emotionally in the key of Meredith's "Love in the Valley." The effect is startling, but I think Scott's poem gains rather than loses by the association. "The Sleeper" stands apart from these other poems in that it is almost unknown. It appeared in Scott's first book, but it was not included in the collected edition and has not appeared in any anthology. It is fragile and it seems in its opening to be only another echo of Tennyson's earliest style, so the hasty reader may miss the originality and truth of the poem. Actually, a profound perception about the nature and beauty of innocence is expressed and in an imagery that is enticing both for what it reveals and for what it hides. The poem begins by telling how "Touched with some divine repose, Isabelle has fallen asleep," and the first three stanzas describe the hushed and enraptured loveliness of the sleeping girl, her spirit calmed by a happy dream:

> Then upfloats a planet strange,
>     Not the moon that mortals know,
> With a magic mountain range,
>     Cones and craters white as snow;
>
> Something different yet the same—
>     Rain by rainbows glorified,
> Roses lit with lambent flame—
>     'Tis the maid moon's other side.
>
> When the sleeper floats from sleep,
>     She will smile the vision o'er,
> See the veined valleys deep,
>     No one ever saw before.
>
> Yet the moon is not betrayed,
>     (Ah! the subtle Isabelle!)
> She's a maiden, and a maid
>     Maiden secrets will not tell.

This, as I have said, is a very fragile poem. It comes dangerously near to being coy, but it is saved by the essential truth of its perception (which is, I take it, that innocence is a form of arcane knowledge that cannot be revealed to the profane.) If the spirit of the youthful Tennyson is here, so is that of Hans Anderson. And so is that of Dr. Freud.

Of the poems in the calmer and more classical strain there are many, and it is hard to select a few that stand far above the rest. Any selection of them would be sure to include "Off Rivière du Loup;" "In the Country Churchyard", an elegy in memory of his father; "Variations on a Seventh Century Theme"; and "The Closed Door", a lovely requiem for his daughter.

## III

The most original of Duncan Campbell Scott's poems are those in which there is a union of these two qualities, emotional intensity and perfection of form; and these, as might have been expected, are the lyrics and ballads of Indian life. For the greater part of his life Duncan Campbell Scott served in the federal Department of Indian Affairs, being the Deputy Superintendent General for almost twenty years. His experiences in this post—his duties sometimes took him on arduous canoe trips into the Indian country south of Hudson Bay—gave him a knowledge of the Indian and his feelings that make his interpretations of the red man unique in our literature. His imagination in the first instance caught and communicated the feel of the vast northern land and peopled it with the survivors of its aboriginal inhabitants; and his knowledge and sympathy saw them, and his art presented them, as human beings, as *man*, capable of dramatic and, indeed, of tragic action. Poetic imagination brought as a kind of insight to dwell upon the Indian as he really is gives their unique significance to early successes like "The Half-Breed Girl" and "The Forsaken" and to later, more elaborately worked out, 'modern' narratives like "At Gull Lake: August, 1810" or "A Scene at Lake Manitou." These last stand alone among Canadian poems for their union of anthropological interest and intensely dramatic power. Written in a simple, dignified, and colloquial verse, they tell stories of passion, death, and cruelty that are remarkable for the objectivity with which they are presented and the cumulative power with which they are developed. Both poems deal with a theme that has touched the poet's imagination deeply—the conflict between two cultures, the red man's and the white's, in the divided heart of the Indian or the half breed. "A Scene at Lake Manitou" tells of the reversion of an Indian mother to the ancient gods of her tribe when the prayers and holy water of the priest cannot save her youthful son from death. "At Gull Lake" takes us back more than a hundred years to a scene of passion and cruelty. It is painted in sharp raw colors; the action is quick and fierce.

> The two camps were pitched on the shore,
> The clustered teepees
> Of Tabashaw Chief of the Saulteaux.
> And on the knoll tufted with poplars
> The gray tents of a trader—
> Nairne of the Orkneys.
> Before his tents under the shade of the poplars
> Sat Keejigo, third of the wives
> Of Tabashaw Chief of the Saulteaux;
> Clad in the skins of antelopes

> Broidered with porcupine quills
> Coloured with vivid dyes,
> Vermilion here and there
> In the roots of her hair . . .
> Keejigo daughter of Launay
> The Normandy hunter
> And Oshawan of the Saulteaux.

The love of the half breed girl for the Scottish trader, to whom she offered her body and spirit

> With abject unreasoning passion,
> As Earth abandons herself
> To the sun and the thrust of the lightning,

is etched in a few vivid strokes, and then given its intensest expression in a lyric that suggests perfectly the quality of primitive Indian poetry:

> The flower lives on the prairie,
> The wind in the sky,
> I am here by beloved;
> The wind and the flower.
>
> The crane hides in the sand-hills,
> Where does the wolverine hide?
> I am here my beloved,
> Heart's-blood on the feathers
> The foot caught in the trap.
>
> Take the flower in your hand,
> The wind in your nostrils;
> I am here my beloved;
> Release the captive
> Heal the wound under the feathers

Action is not long delayed, and the lyric gives way to a rapid narrative movement:

> A storm-cloud was marching
> Vast on the prairie . . .
> Twice had Nairne turned her away
> Afraid of the venom of Tabashaw,
> Twice had the Chief fired at his tents
> And now when two bullets
> Whistled above the encampment
> He yelled, "Drive this bitch to her master."

Keejigo went down a path by the lake . . .

At the top of the bank
The old wives caught her and cast her down
Where Tabashaw crouched by his camp-fire.

He snatched a live brand from the embers,
Seared her cheeks,
Blinded her eyes,
Destroyed her beauty with fire,
Screaming, "Take that face to your lover."
Keejigo held her face to the fury
And made no sound.
The old wives dragged her away
And threw her over the bank
Like a dead dog.
Then burst the storm . . .

The poem does not end here. It is dramatic, startling, horrible;
but if it ended here, it would be nothing more than strong melo-
drama. The hardest problem of the artist still remains—to find
the tragic reconciliation of beauty and terror. The final section of
the poem is a symphonic evocation of storm-tossed skies and
forests, followed by retreating clouds, a rainbow, and the setting
sun:

The wind withdrew the veil from the shine of the moon,
She rose changing her dusky shade for the glow
Of the prairie lily, till free of all blemish of colour
She came to her zenith without a cloud or a star,
A lovely perfection, snow-pure in the heaven of midnight.
After the beauty of terror the beauty of peace.

### IV.

We cannot read these beautiful elegiac lines today without
pausing to think of the man who wrote them, whose long and
honourable career has so recently drawn to a close. Like his
friend Lampman, Duncan Campbell Scott has always in a sense
been an elegiac poet. His intense and scholarly poetry every
where shows a consciousness of the limitations, if not the vanity,
of human wishes; and there is present in much of it an awareness of the life-enriching nearness of death. One thinks today of
the lines from "In a Country Churchyard," and perhaps they
will do to end this tribute, for though they come from his earliest

book they are the perfection of his calm and classical style. I
shall not forget that he read them to me in the great booklined
room of his Ottawa house a day or two after his eightieth birthday.

This is the paradise of common things,
  The scourged and trampled here find peace to grow,
  The frost to furrow and the wind to sow,
The mighty sun to time their blossomings;
  And now they keep
A crown reflowering on the tombs of kings
  Who earned their triumph and have claimed their
sleep.

Yea, each is here a prince in his own right,
  Who dwelt disguised amid the multitude,
  And when his time was come, in haughty mood,
Shook off his motley and reclaimed his might;
  His sombre throne
In the vast province of perpetual night,
  He holds secure, inviolate, alone.

The poor forgets that ever he was poor,
  The priest has lost his science of the truth,
  The maid her beauty, and the youth his youth;
The statesman has forgot his subtle lure,
  The old his age,
The sick his suffering, and the leech his cure,
  The poet his perplexed and vacant page ...

But better for my purpose than this—distinguished and beautiful
as these verses are—is the fine elegy in prose with which Duncan
Campbell Scott closed his *Memoir* of his friend and fellow poet,
his peer and companion, Archibald Lampman:

He rests in Beechwood Cemetery, part of the wild wood
through which he was accustomed to wander speering about
the chilly margin of snow-water pools for the first spring
flowers. He said it was a good spot in which to lie when all
was over with life. Even if there be no sense in these houses
of shade, it is a pleasant foreknowledge to be aware that
above one's unrealizing head the snow will sift, the small
ferns rise and the birds come back in nesting-time. And
though he be forever rapt from such things, careless of them
and unaware, the sternest wind from under the pole star

will blow unconfined over his grave, about it the first hepaticas will gather in fragile companies, the vesper sparrow will return to nest in the grass, and from a branch of maple to sing in the cool dusk.

Here with this epitaph, which might have come from the *Greek Anthology*, let us take farewell of the last, and not the least, of our poets of the Golden Age.

# Refining Fire:
# The Meaning and Use of Poetry
## 1954

In approaching the problem of what a poem is, what is means, or what is communicates, I would ask you to put out of your minds any preconceived opinions about the nature, purposes, or methods of poetry. Put aside if you can such arbitrary generalizations about the nature of poetry as that it is, or ought to be, emotional; that it must be 'elevated'; it must be 'beautiful'; it must deal with 'poetic' subjects. Where these notions are not too hopelessly vague, they have validity, but their main tendency is to limit and dilute our appreciation and cloud our understanding. The subject matter of poetry is much wider in scope, more immediate and less selective, much less respectable and much more intense than most of us realize.

Let us think of a poem rather than of poetry; and let us attempt a working definition. It might go something like this. A poem is a highly organized, complex, and unified re-creation of experience in which the maximum use of meaning and suggestion in the sounds of words has been achieved with the minimum essential outlay of words. A poem is not the description of an experience, it is itself an experience, and it awakens in the mind of the alert and receptive reader a new experience analogous to the one in the mind of the poet ultimately responsible for the creation of the poem. The more sensitive the reader and the better instructed he is the closer will his experience be to that of the poet. It is almost as difficult, and quite as important, to be a good reader as to be a good poet.

Yet it is not, I would like to maintain, the nature of the experience, or the moral respectability of the emotions that produced it or rose out of it, or even the immediate, practical, sentimental consequences that appear to flow from it, that make a poem good rather than bad or valuable rather than dangerous. Too often a poem is thought to achieve morality and usefulness and *does* achieve popularity through an unconsciously hypocritical failure to pierce uncompromisingly through to the heart of an experience which would have become too bitter and too painful had the poet dared to descend more deeply into it. The great poets are those who have dared to descend more deeply into the heart of reality, and some of them have found the way there through the emotions of hate, fear, lust, anger, and despair. The names of Raleigh, Donne, Pope, Swift, Hardy, and the author of *Lear* are not the least honoured among poets.

At this point we must ask: If the worth of a poem is not to be found in the nature of the re-created experience or in the morality or cheerfulness of its resolution, where is it to be found? Upon what does it depend?

The answer is that the value of a poem lies in the intensity with which an experience has been encountered, and the accuracy with which its consequences, good or evil, delightful or painful, have been recognized and accepted. It is the integrity, the clarity, and the completeness with which an experience is met, whether it is trivial, harsh, ugly, magnificent, or delightful, that counts in the evaluation not only of a poem's goodness but also of its usefulness. The nature of the experience, as such, has nothing to do with the genuineness or the goodness of the poem, and no preconceived opinion can postulate the special conditions under which the right intensity of pressure will be generated.

It follows that there are no "poetic" subjects. Any subject, no matter how unpromising, can be made the source of poetry when shaped by the poetic imagination. Accuracy of perception and concentrated clarity of expression—what might, in its finest manifestation, be called "nakedness of vision"—can make the humblest and even the vilest material a source of poetry, so that a poem is not only a recreation of experience but also a transfiguration of experience, or in Joycean terms, an epiphany.

Let me cite a particular example to demonstrate *what is done* in a poem and also, in part, *how* it is done. Here is a poem of eight lines by the contemporary American poet William Carlos Williams in which with remarkable concentration we are given a new and surprising vision of something we may have often looked at but have never actually seen with the eye of the imagination until the poet showed it to us. It is called—

*Flowers by the Sea*
When over the flowery sharp pasture's
edge, unseen, the salt ocean

lifts its form—chickory and daisies
tied, released, seem hardly flowers alone

but color and the movement—or the shape
perhaps—of restlessness, whereas

the sea is circled and sways
peacefully upon its plantlike stem

Brief and clear as it is, this little poem states, or, rather, illustrates, a paradox—the paradox that the sea and the pasture each
suggests the other's basic nature rather than its own. But the
curious thing is that the unexpected reversal of images which
makes the point of the poem emerges suddenly, only after we
have absorbed the whole dazzling picture of the sunny windswept seaside field and felt the tousled salt-laden atmosphere of
the summer day. The first unexpected identification is that of the
restless amalgam of colour and movement in the flowers and
grasses—"the shape, perhaps, of restlessness"—with the ebb and
flow ("tied, released") of the waves; and, parallel to it, but much
richer and grander, is the sudden awareness of the vast blue
round of the ocean itself, swaying like an enormous flower.
There has indeed been a sea-change into something rich and
strange, and, most daringly, the magic has been performed in
the realm of the familiar, not in that of the exotic.

*Flowers by the Sea* expresses an experience, which culminates
for both poet and reader in the intuitive flash at the close, when
it is perceived not that the flowers and the sea are like one
another in some respects but that the flowers *are* a sea and the
sea *is* a flower. The imagination leaves out all but the common
qualities shared by the flowers and the waves, all but colour and
movement, that is—all but the blue circular shape and the swaying motion. Here intense concentration upon what the senses
and the imagination have isolated leads to a form of truth that is
more limited but more precious than the truth of science or fact,
for it is a truth perceived simultaneously by the heart, the imagination, and the mind. In this poem sense impressions received
from the fluid, elusively beautiful object of attention seem all
important. And they *are* all important, but not—even in a poem
so self-contained and self-justifying as this one—for themselves
alone, or as the generating source of emotion. What gives the
poem its point and its tang is the paradoxical reversal of ordinary experience, when in a flash the flowers are seen as a sea
and the sea as a flower—and this is an *intellectual* act. Although
what touches the emotions here is first, the evocation of all the
delight that gathers round the sunny windswept landscape of

flowers by the dancing sea, it is finally the exhilaration that accompanies the perception of a paradox. Not in metaphysical poetry only does intellectual action, whether slowly or swiftly brought to a consummation, resolve itself in emotion when it comes to its successful and dramatic conclusion.

These considerations have carried us far away from the popular conception of poetry as something flowery, vague, and conventional in a "nice" and undisturbing way. If that widespread conception were at all true, poetry would of course be much simpler than it is—and much less interesting. It would be like any other gesture or experience that lacked passion, originality, or intelligent direction. Not such easy things as vagueness and "niceness" but difficult things—precision and intensity—are the marks of the genuine in poetry.

It is true, however, that these marks of the genuine are to be found in two sharply contrasted types of poetry: the positive, traditional poetry which we easily recognize as universal and optimistic; and the negative, unorthodox poetry that tells unpleasant truths. Both kinds are true and valuable in their separate ways, and indeed there are many instances of a poet's writing in both moods at different times, and occasionally, in the same work. Let us briefly consider each in turn.

Poetry, certainly, most often expresses ideas and emotions felt generally by all mankind to be true in the long run to the common experience of humanity. Such poetry is simple, affirmative, conservative, "acceptable," and genuinely popular. It does not make its appeal by its originality or its unexpectedness, or even by its profundity, but by its convincing rightness, by the *felt* truth with which it confirms people in what they have come to feel and believe without ever having been able to put it into memorable words. This is the idea of Pope's classical conception of poetry as "What oft was thought but ne'er so well expressed" and of Keats' well-known statement: "I think poetry should surprise by a fine excess, and not by singularity. It should strike the reader as a wording of his own highest thoughts, and appear almost a remembrance."

Poems and images fitting these descriptions are immediately satisfying; they are accepted at once and never forgotten. Lines whose impressiveness are of this order are the easiest to call to mind:

> She walks in beauty like the night
>
> [Byron]

I wandered lonely as a cloud

[Wordsworth]


The day is done and the darkness
  Falls from the wings of night
As a feather is wafted downward
  From an eagle in his flight.

[Longfellow]


The uncertain glory of an April day

[Shakespeare]


The rightness and what one might perhaps call the unviolent nostalgia of these images are among the chief factors contributing to their effectiveness. Good popular poetry derives its strength from the fact that it soothes and reassures rather than challenges and surprises us. The attitude toward experience and the evaluation of it are in harmony with the most commonly accepted and generally valid views of mankind.

But the poet has always had another function to perform. His eye is sharper than that of the ordinary person, and like the prophet—or, as Louis MacNeice has said, like the informer—he has always made it part of his business to see the "other side" of things and to present feelings and attitudes that shock or undermine everything that has been too complacently accepted. Images and poems in this mode are not necessarily more difficult to understand than those in the mode of "acceptance." But it is perhaps more difficult for the poet of the unusual and the unaccepted to overcome the prejudices of his readers and to force a recognition of what had hitherto been hidden or repressed.

This distinction between the two types of poetry—that which confirms and reassures and that which shocks or disturbs—extends to the style itself, especially to the handling of images and figurative language. If we place beside the beautiful lines just quoted parallel images of this second kind, we discover that in the latter group the distance between the two arms of the comparison (between, for instance, the brightness of God and the depth of darkness in the first quotation below) is much greater; the things compared in a simile or identified in a metaphor are not nearly so easily seen to be alike. And the effect is not to confirm us in what we already feel but to startle us awake so that we become aware of something not experienced before:

> There is in God (some say)
> A deep but dazzling darkness.
>
> [Henry Vaughan]

> I should have been a pair of ragged claws
> Scuttling across the floors of silent seas.
>
> [Eliot]

> The fine fine wind that takes its course through
>       the chaos of the world
> Like an exquisite chisel, a wedgeblade inserted. . . .
>
> [D. H. Lawrence]

> A serpent swam a vertex to the sun
>       On unpaced beaches leaned its
>         tongue and drummed.
> What fountains did I hear? What icy speeches?
>
> [Hart Crane]

> April is the cruelest month. . . .
>
> [Eliot]

Lines like these, and the poems they are taken from, reveal the poet in his most valuable rôle—as the uncoverer of the hidden secrets of the human consciousness and as the conscience of society.

I shall develop this point in a moment, but first I wish to mitigate its seeming harshness. Nó matter how subversive of human self-esteem, how disillusioned or bitter a poet's philosophical outlook may be, it is always delight and love that are at the heart of his writing, idealizing the world of sensation and making it human. This delight and love are first and foremost a passion of the eye, a sort of visual thirst that drinks eagerly whatever it lights upon:

> Eye, gazelle, delicate wanderer, drinker of horizon's fluid
> line

—as Stephen Spender has expressed it: and accuracy and vividness are never sacrificed to ornament or faked emotion—at least in genuine poetry they are not. Accuracy, which is a kind of faithfulness and sincerity, is one of the special marks of high excellence. Consider Browning's

> The wild tulip at end of its tube blows out its great red bell
> Like a thin clear bubble of blood

or Whitman's

> Earth of the vitreous pour of the full moon just tinged
>     with blue!
> Earth of shine and dark mottling the tide of the river!

or Herrick's synthesis of several of the sense impressions:

> Whenas in silks my *Julia* goes,
> Then, then, methinks, how sweetly flowes
> The liquefaction of her clothes.
>
> Next, when I cast mine eyes and see
> That brave Vibration each way free;
> O how that glittering taketh me!

or Marianne Moore's curiously comparable sound-picture, as she describes a ship's boat moving over the ocean:

> —the blades of the oars
> moving together like the feet of water-spiders. . . .
> The wrinkles progress upon themselves in a phalanx—
> beautiful
>     under networks of foam
> and fade breathlessly while the sea rustles in and out of the
>     seaweed . . .

Each of these passages illustrates in its own way how the poet looks at, and listens to the world around him, transmuting it with the glow of his own delight into that "golden" realm of Sir Philip Sidney declared to be beyond nature.


What, it is time to ask, is the special, unique, and characteristic use of the perceptiveness and accuracy with which a poet responds to experience?—*use*, I mean, to the reader? and to society?

Its first and most fundamental use—first and most fundamental because all other possible uses must come through or grow out of this one—is the training, developing, exercising, and strengthening of the sensibilities themselves, so that our perceptions of physical things are made at once sharper, subtler, more penetrating and also stronger and more intense. And, in turn, in the well-tempered personality, the training of poetry and art helps to develop a corresponding purification and strengthening of the emotional and intellectual faculties.

This is why the neglect or perversion of criticism in our schools and colleges, and indeed in our culture generally, is so serious a matter. We have forgotten, or perhaps have not yet fully realized, that the reading of imaginative literature is itself an art—both a fine art and a useful art—an art that involves perception, apprehension, and evaluation, and that to neglect it or merely to pay it lip-service or to substitute vague appreciation for the hard work and discipline that is involved in the technique of accurate reading—to do any of these things is to corrupt the spiritual life of the community. Today we have special problems. As the dramatic critic, Eric Bentley, wrote recently: "We have destroyed the old aristocratic culture, which, for all its faults had a place for the arts, and have created a culture of commodities, which to be sure, has a place for everything—upon one condition: that everything become a commodity. Thus there is one sort of literature that flourishes today as never before: commodity literature as promoted by the book clubs and publishers' salesmen."

This same point of view has been behind the critical activity of Mr. F. R. Leavis and his group of scholars and critics at Cambridge. In the first issue of their magazine *Scrutiny* in 1932, Mr. Leavis spoke for those who see a connection between the plight of the arts in the modern world and the present drift of civilization. The arts, he affirmed, are more than a luxury product. He described them in Arnoldian terms as "the storehouse of recorded values," and went on to say in a sentence whose validity I have assumed throughout this essay, that "There is a necessary relationship between the quality of an individual's response to art and his general fitness for humane existence." Another of the Cambridge school of scholar-critics, Mr. L. C. Knights, has stressed the value for the humanities of the discipline involved in the perceptive study of literature. "The reading of literature, insofar as it is anything more than a pastime," declares Mr. Knights, "involves the continuous development of the power of intelligent discrimination. Literature, moreover, is simply the exact expression of realized values. It is part of the artist's function to give precise meaning to ideas and sentiments that are only obscurely perceived by his contemporaries."

This conception of the poet's function is in harmony with what I was saying earlier about the poet and artist as prophet, medicineman, and informer. I pick up the word "informer" from Louis MacNeice, who speaks of the poet as a blend of the informer and the entertainer. He means "informer" in the "bad" sense of the word. The poet is one who *tells on us*. He is our secret conscience. He reveals hidden and uncomfortable truths. He lets light and air into dark, closed places. He pricks the wounds of the unconscious and prevents them from festering. He exposes suppressed evil, and can make us whole again.

The same thought is expressed as the climactic idea in R. G. Collingwood's great work, *The Principles of Art*. After an acute analysis of one of the greatest and most representative of modern masterpieces, T. S. Eliot's *The Waste Land*, Collingwood brings his study of art to a conclusion with the following pertinent summary:

"To readers who want not amusement or magic, but poetry, and who want to know what poetry can be if it is to be neither of these things, *The Waste Land* supplies an answer. And by reflecting on it we can perhaps detect one more characteristic which art must have, if it is to forgo both entertainment-value and magical value, and draw a subject matter from its audience themselves. It must be prophetic. The artist must prophesy not in the sense that he foretells things to come, but in the sense that he tells his audience, at risk of their displeasure, the secrets of their own hearts. His business as an artist is to speak out, to make a clean breast. But what he has to utter is not, as the individualistic theory of art would have us think, his own secrets. As spokesman of his community, the secrets he must utter are theirs. The reason why they need him is that no community altogether knows its own heart; and by failing in this knowledge a community deceives itself on the one subject concerning which ignorance means death. For the evils which come from that ignorance the poet as prophet suggests no remedy, because he has already given one. The remedy is the poem itself. Art is the community's medicine for the worst disease of mind, the corruption of consciousness." Poetry, we may add, is the prime and essential art in the performance of this function, for the poet makes us re-examine our perceptions and teaches us to keep our words and therefore our ideas, clean and precise.

The perceptive reading of poetry, then — an activity which involves the discipline of criticism but which always must return to pleasure and delight — is seen as a useful action. It has a practical value, and it involves an interplay not only between the poet as an individual and the individual reader but between both and the community. Shelley was aware of this when he wrote in his *Defence of Poetry*: "A man to be greatly good, must imagine intensely and comprehensively; he must put himself in the place of another and of many others; the pains and pleasures of his species must become his own . . . Whatever strengthens and purifies the affections, enlarges the imagination, and adds spirit to sense, is useful." Never more useful—do I need to add?—than here and now, in the present crisis of world affairs, when as the Anglo-American poet, W. H. Auden, has put it, "We must love one another or die."

Professor Collingwood, who was a philosopher and a historian, boldly extended the realm of the classic to include the masterpieces of our own time. This is only proper. To be afraid to do so is to impugn the validity of your critical principles and indeed of your scholarship. And it is to be something considerably less than completely useful. For it is also the task of scholarship and criticism to discover, explore, and evaluate the modern work that lifts itself above the ordinary and pushing back into the past and forward into the future, proclaims itself a classic.

Are there none such? Can we not discern them? Can we not apply the same standards of measurement that time and the scholar-critics have applied to the classics of the past (clarity, wholeness, integrity, depth, intensity, universality) and separate the works of permanent excellence from the slick, the exciting, the charming, or the meretricious? At least we must try. And so, to conclude, I shall attempt to sum up briefly what we may learn about the terrible age we live in from the testimony of the great modern classics of the creative imagination.

A consideration of these reveals a common rejection of objective realism as a literary method and of social amelioration as an end. The causes of the decay of civilization as expressed in the poetry of Eliot and the fiction of Proust and Joyce are seen to be metaphysical and religious—the result of ways of feeling and habits of mind produced by the mechanization of the surface of life and the secularization of thought. In reaction to this, the modern masters have sought the recovery of myth and in some cases of dogma: in Yeats an esoteric and eclectic magical dogma, in Eliot a catholic and Christian one. As Northrop Frye has written: "The age that produced the hell of Rimbaud and the angels of Rilke, Kafka's castle and James's ivory tower, the spirals of Yeats and the hermaphrodites of Proust, the intricate dying-god symbolism attached to Christ in Eliot and the exhaustive treatment of Old Testament myths in Mann's study of Joseph, is once again a great mythapoeic age." The work of the reestablishment of order has begun by the analysis of a dying chaos in *Ulysses* and *Remembrance of Things Past* and by the exploration of the moral confusion of our time in Gide and James and Kafka. All these masters of the creative imagination, these *poets* whether they write in prose or verse, are united in a common task, and they are in agreement with their nineteenth century forerunners, Dostoievsky, Baudelaire, and Rimbaud that the heart of the matter lies in the problem of guilt and suffering. The wisdom to be derived in the final analysis from modern imaginative literature is that responsibility must be accepted once more as a spiritual reality before the individual can be restored to grace or society to civilization. Although the picture that emerges from the great prophetic literature of our time is one of isolation, horror, and suffering, the suffering has been wilfully and consciously entered into by the creative imagination. "In the destructive element immerse: that is the way."

But the modern world is not Hell; the suffering is not eternal nor infinite nor hopeless. It is rather the refining fire into which Arnaut Daniel in the *Purgatorio* dived back, because, as he said to Virgil, "I see with joy the day for which I hope before me."

# A SALUTE TO LAYTON
## In Praise of his Earliest Masterpieces

### 1956

In 1954 Irving Layton published two volumes of verse that stood out as remarkable in a year that was distinguished by several books of more than usual merit, including new collections by P. K. Page and F. R. Scott : One of Mr. Layton's books, *The Long Pea-shooter*, was mainly satirical; the other *In the Midst of my Fever*, was entirely serious, though not at all solemn. It contained a number of poems that are not only far above anything he has done before but are as fine as any written by a poet of Mr. Layton's generation in America.

This year Mr. Layton has also published two volumes; and again one is chiefly satirical (*The Blue Propeller*) while the other (*The Cold Green Element*) is lyrical and dramatic. Neither of these books seems to me quite as good as its predecessor, though *The Cold Green Element* has so much in it that is both original and excellent that it stands out as the most remarkable achievement of another very fruitful year in Canadian poetry.

The most prolific and perhaps the most fluent Canadian poet since Bliss Carman, Layton has published eight privately printed volumes since 1945 and has fought a continuous running engagement with reviewers and critics. The opposition or neglect his early work encountered is not to be attributed entirely to stupidity or cowardice on the part of the reviewers. It would have required second-sight, or friendly partiality, to foretell from the poetry he published before 1954 the high order of excellence shown by *In the Midst of my Fever* and *The Gold Green Element*, and there was much in the earlier books (as there is a little in the later) which seemed arrogant, puerile, or deliberately offensive. Mr. Layton set himself up as a demolisher of the genteel tradition—in itself a worthy enough undertaking, heaven knows—but it is not so easy to succeed in as the enthusiast hopes. To make any real progress in it requires a measure of sophistication and humility that Mr. Layton achieves in his two best books but which is conspicuously absent from the early ones, and not too evident in his avowedly satirical ones, where perhaps sophistication and humility are most needed. Wherever Mr. Layton has

been least successful one discovers a petulant fascination with
sexual and functional processes and a childish flaunting of four-
letter words that seem to be flung about with an angry rather
than a joyous abandon. Northrop Frye, writing in *Letters in
Canada: 1951*, named the weaknesses exactly, though unlike any
other critic outside Mr. Layton's circle of devoted friends he
looked sharply and closely enough to detect the outlines of the
real poet who was later to emerge. "The idea in Mr. Layton's
poetry," wrote Frye, "is to use an intensely personal imagination
as an edged tool against a world cemented by smugness, hacking
and chopping with a sharp image here, an acid comment there,
trying to find holes and weak spots where the free mind can
enroot and sprout. It is the misfortune of this technique that the
successes are quiet and the faults raucous. There is a real poet
buried in Mr. Layton. . . . But where the imagination is conceived
as militant, there is apt to develop a split between what the poet
can write and what he thinks he ought to write for his cause.
Most of Mr. Layton's book [*The Back Huntsman*] is the work,
not of the poet in him, but of a noisy hot-gospeller who has no
real respect for poetry. . . . One can get as tired of buttocks in Mr.
Layton as of buttercups in the *Canadian Poetry Magazine*; and a
poet whose imagination is still fettered by a moral conscience,
even an anti-conventional one, gives the impression of being in
the same state of bondage as the society he attacks."

I quote this adverse criticism partly because I agree with the
main tenour of it, though I regret (and I imagine Mr. Frye
perhaps regrets) the phrase about "no real respect for poetry,"
but chiefly in order to show how far Mr. Layton has come in the
two masterful volumes of 1954 and 1955. Mr. Layton, it is clear,
has been one of those poets who has to write too much in order
to be able to write at all. He loves everything he writes, even the
unsuccessful experiments—perhaps most of all the unsuccessful
experiments, as a mother loves the ugly child best—and instead
of throwing them in the waste basket or filing them away for
future revision, he swells a volume with them. But this habit, if it
has been hard on the reader, has been good for the poet. Practice in his craft has now made him well nigh perfect, at least in a
score of superb poems. The self-confidence that looked like arrogance in the early verse and the savage indignation that
looked like mere contempt have ripened in quality and grown in
sharpness. In the new success imagery and rhythm alike have
taken on a precise and exciting inevitability that testified to a
technical virtuosity that only a very skilful critic could have
foreseen from the early volumes. In fairness both to Mr. Layton

and Mr. Frye, I must recall a few sentences from a later review, Mr. Frye's notice of *In the Midst of my Fever* in *Letters in Canada: 1954* " ... The question of whether Mr. Layton is a real poet is settled.... An imaginative revolution is proclaimed all through this book: when he says that 'something has taught me severity, exactness of speech' or 'has given me a turn for sculptured stone,' we see a new excitement and intensity in the process of writing. At last it is possible to see what kind of poet Mr. Layton is, and he proves to be not a satirist at all, but an erudite elegaic poet, whose technique turns on an aligning of the romantic and the ironic. ... "

What more precisely, it is time to ask, are the qualities which especially distinguish *The Cold Green Element*, as they did *In the Midst of my Fever*? To describe them it is necessary to separate them, though it is their final overall and unified effect that gives them their significance. I would single out first a mastery of rhythm, which controls the speed and direction of emotional intensity within an often elaborate and formal stanza pattern. In such poems as *Composition in Late Spring, Metzinger: Girl with A Bird,* or *The Birth of Tragedy* in the earlier volume, and *Boys in October, the Cold Green Element, Orpheus,* or *I would for your sake be gentle* in the later, there is an unmistakable fluctuation of thought and feeling that rises in part from the metrical rightness of phrase, sentence, and paragraph. This is verse that is as well-written as prose; but even in its most homely and familiar moods it is never prosaic. The prevailing rhythms are speech, and the diction generally is colloquial. But when necessary—at climactic moments that seem to be selected with a lucky rightness—language and rhythm take on a richness and emphasis that gives an effect that is sometimes purely lyrical and sometimes has a classic and monumental stillness. Any of the poems above will illustrate the lyrical or dramatic movement that flows consistently and variously through whirls and eddies to an often surprising but perfectly right conclusion. Here is one of the shortest, *Boys in October*:

> Like Barbarossa's beard bright with oil
> The maples glisten with the season's rain;
> The day's porous, as October days are,
> And objects have more space about them.
>
> All field things seem weightless, abstract,
> As if they'd taken one step back
> To see themselves as they literally are
> After the dementia of summer.

Now hale and sinewy my son, his friend
(The construction sand making a kind of
Festival under their feet) in their
Absorbed arm-on-shoulder stance

Look I think for all the world
Like some antique couple in a wood
Whom unexpected sibyls have made rich
(Something perhaps dressed up by Ovid)

On one condition, alas:
they'll not use
The gold but hold it as a memorial
To Chance and their own abstinence.

The naturalness and originality of the observation shown here
(especially remarkable in the second stanza) are virtues that go
deeper than technical accomplishment and come from the sensibility and character of the poet. The technical virtuosity, of
course, does itself rise out of feelings and convictions about the
significance of experience and the place of man in nature and
society. As a result, the poems are rooted in a personal here and
now, and emotion and thought grow out of physical sensation.
Mr. Layton has taken to heart the dictum of his master, William
Carlos Williams: "Say it: no ideas but in things"—which doesn't
mean "no ideas". These poems are full of ideas: but they are
ideas which emerge from the whole being, which includes, we
are constantly reminded, the glands, pores, muscles, nerve
centres, and ganglia, as well as the mind that organizes, even if it
cannot always control or command. After Whitman and Lawrence it has become possible for a poet of Mr. Layton's generation to take the physical side of our nature for granted and write
about it without fuss or apology as a conditioning factor in
emotion and thought. Possible—but not easy, as the false starts
among Layton's early poems testify. A consequence of the new
wholeness, which some of the best of the later poems, *Bacchanal,
Latria, For Louise, age 17,* and *Love's Diffidence,* identify with
the old, classic pagan wholeness, is an escape from the shadow
of repression and fear into the sunlight of a genuine freedom.
For Mr. Layton this has made poetry possible and has not only
enabled him to write good poems but to understand the nature
of the poetic process itself. One of the most enlightening and
successful of the pieces in *The Cold Green Element* is a fruit of
this understanding; its title, indeed, is *The Poetic Process.* It is
too long to quote here, but I recommend it to the reader who

wants both an explicit statement and a concrete illustration of what Mr. Layton means by poetry and what he believes it can and should do.

There are other virtues in these poems that I haven't got around to naming yet: a surprising variety of seemingly incompatible images all made relevant and put to use; a power to generate fantasy out of reality without ever leaving reality behind; and a pervasive hard-to-define quality that shows itself most clearly in the phrasing, though it is in the structure of the best poems too: I can only name it *elegance*. It can be easily and briefly illustrated. First in single lines or phrases: "the furies clear a path for me to the worm"; "in the morning-light the windows shone like saints pleased with the genius that had painted them"; "A quiet madman, never far from tears." Next in stanzas—as these that form the last half of *The Cold Green Element* and illustrate not only Layton's elegance but the other qualities I have been speaking of as well:

> The ailments escaped from the labels
> of medicine bottles are all fled to the wind;
> I've seen myself lately in the eyes
>         of old women,
> spent streams mourning my manhood,
>
> in whose old pupils the sun became
> a bloodsmear on broad catalpa leaves
> and hanging from ancient twigs,
>         my murdered selves
> sparked the air like the muted collisions
>
> of fruit. A black dog howls down my blood,
> a black dog with yellow eyes;
> he too by someone's inadvertence
>         saw the bloodsmear
> on the broad catalpa leaves.
>
> But the furies clear a path for me to the worm
> who sang for an hour in the throat of a robin,
> and misled by the cries of young boys
>         I am again
> a breathless swimmer in that cold green element.

Our pleasure here depends on many things: the elegance of the writing, the neatness of the stanza-pattern, the aptness of the imagery, and the mythmaking creativeness that draws its materials as easily from drugstore shelves as from the great classic tale of Orpheus. Like this poem, the best score of pieces in these four volumes signal the arrival of one of the finest poets of the modern revival in Canada. The new unpublished poems Mr. Layton read at the Writers' Conference at Kingston last summer indicate that there is to be no let-up in his stream of productivity. For this I, for one, am very grateful.

# Introduction to *The Blasted Pine*:

## An Anthology of Satire, Invective, and Disrespectful Verse chiefly by Canadian Poets, Selected and Arranged by F. R. Scott and A. J. H. Smith

## 1957

### I

"Satire, invective, and disrespectful verse" describes accurately enough what may seem to some readers a rather curious mixture of poetry, doggerel, light verse, comic rhymes, and well aimed spitballs. Traditionally, satire and invective are a method of exposing folly to the ridicule of reasonable men and vice to the condemnation of virtuous and responsible men. John Dryden put it well when he wrote, "The true end of satire is the amendment of vice by correction" (i.e., by administration of the cane), but he added a necessary reminder when he continued, "He who writes honestly is no more an enemy to the offender, than the physician to the patient, when he prescribes harsh remedies to an inveterate disease."

This is the justification of most of the pieces collected here. All of them, or nearly all of them—there are a few amusing, ridiculous, or delightful "sports" that fall outside our categories —are sharply critical, in one way or another, of some aspect of Canadian life that has more often been accepted uncritically. They have been chosen because they sound a sour note. Their tone is harsh, sometimes unrefined, sometimes, perhaps, distorted, but always unsentimental—the noise that common sense makes, or the whisper of intelligence. It is a note which has generally been drowned out in the diapason of praise with which Canadian poets have hymned the glories of the True North Strong and Free.

The voice of the dissenter, however, has never been quite silent. It has always performed the useful function of an opposition party—though of necessity not a loyal one. The first function of the kind of criticism that is immediately useful in the early stages of any reform, whether in the field of morals, manners, social customs, or politics, is to be *destructive*. Constructive criticism is all very well at a later stage, or if the thing criticized is merely superficial—error, not sin. But the most effective attack is the sharpest attack. Intensity, bitterness, and passion, then, are the qualities by which the excellence of satire and invective is to be measured. A kind of rough strength and a personal tang—the body odour of indignation—give a validity and virtue even to crude rhymes and popular doggerel.

The force of this collection is strengthened by the wide net we have drawn. Amateur writers, men of affairs, journalists, politicians, and plain people—farmers, settlers, business men, and (more recently) professors—are here, along with the established poets. And while there are a number of beautiful and deeply-felt pieces that are excellent as poetry (Lampman's *City of the End of Things*, Marriott's *Prairie Graveyard*, Mandel's *Estevan, Saskatchewan*, to name the first that come to mind) there are many that derive their strength from being nothing more than they frankly proclaim themselves to be—comic, grotesque, or simply casual. There are a few things here too that nobody would maintain are anything but bad poetry. But there is bad poetry, and bad poetry; and there is such a thing as "good" bad poetry. The verses by O'Grady, McLachlan, and Glendinning in the early days are sometimes of this sort. So are those by their close relative, Sarah Binks. They are as well worth reading as the more vaporous rhapsodies of the Maple Leaf school of patriotic nature poets.

The student of Canadian history will discover a curious truth if he places these verses in their historical setting. He will discover that it is the critics, objectors, and nay-sayers, not the conformists, who are most often in advance of their time, who most accurately foreshadow new developments and point the direction in which the reluctant conservative is going to be dragged. The reason is that the malcontent is almost invariably a realist, with his eye fixed steadily on a concrete grievance, while the cheerful enthusiast is generally a sentimental idealist. There are exceptions, of course. But one of the most genuine sources of interest in a collection like this is the opportunity it gives us of watching the operations of the critical spirit throughout nearly a century and a half of our national development. There is in these pages a brief history of Canadian thought; the poems expose an idea or a form of behaviour to public ridicule, and at the same time assert the superiority of the alternative view implied by the attack. For this reason the time of original publication of each poem is important; opinions which today seem dated or even quaint are of interest when they first appear in their historical context.

## II

The critical spirit, when it finds expression in satire and invective, may be distinguished by its point of view, purpose, and direction of aim, into one of two classes: the classical or conservative, and the romantic or revolutionary. The satirist in a classical age directs his wit or anger against the non-conformist, the sectarian, and the eccentric — against all, that is who diverge from the norm of rational behaviour and social agreeableness. In an age of well established order everybody knows what this is. The satirist then is orthodox and respectable, an exponent of fixed and generally respected principles of right feeling, correct thinking, and proper behaviour. Such satire is not likely to develop very strongly in a colony, except in the hands of a few Tory administrators, wealthy land-holders, and Church-of-England clergymen in the earliest period.

In a time of social change, such as occurred with the industrial revolution and the romantic revival (strange but inevitable concatenation!) or after World War I and the Great Depression, satire launches its attack from a different point of view, at a different target, and with a different purpose. It is now the turn of the Individualist, the revolutionary, and the eccentric; and he pits himself against the established system of convention and privilege. No longer the voice of society and reason, he is one crying in the wilderness, and his critical intelligence and righteous indignation shine like bright lamps in a bleak world. It is satire of this sort that we shall find mainly, though not quite exclusively, in this book. It is the voice of a few isolated, sharp-sighted, sharp-tongued plain-speakers that we hear most often chastising, complaining, declaiming or singing in the following pages. It is a little surprising that there have not been more of them.

We are a new country asserting its individuality against the traditions of the past. Is not the act of emigration itself a kind of satire — a romantic, indeed a revolutionary rejection of an established order? The emigrant discards an old life in favour of another to be established in a new land. Yet the English and Scottish emigrants from the Old Country — to say nothing of the United Empire Loyalists — were usually just that — emigrants, not immigrants, and the efforts they made in their new home to imitate and re-establish the attitudes and habits of the old have given to later generations of Canadian their most truly national subject of satire and irony. This accounts for the presence here of so much criticism of bourgeois respectability, Tory imperialism, mercantile or sectarian hypocrisy, and complacent materialism.

What almost all our satirists stand against is conformity of one kind or another. The verses included here, whether satirical or not, are pessimistic and destructive, and whether on a personal, social, or metaphysical level, they are all subversive—distinguished by an absence of that helpful, optimistic cheerfulness that is generally thought to be a duty nowadays. The poets and versifiers we have brought together are men who have looked behind the façade of conventional acceptance and—in most of these poems at least—have refused to play the game. In doing so, they have taken what we are compelled to describe, in old-fashioned terms, as a moral stand.

All satire, indeed, and most invective, is moral: it asserts or implies a standard of value. It makes judgments, and demands or seizes the right of self-assertion. It takes sides, speaks out, and enters actively into social, political, or moral engagements. It is a form of action, and its writers are partisans. They are very much needed in Canada today—and tomorrow.

As we wrote these lines our eyes fell on a paragraph in the *Canadian Forum* for March 1957. We write it into the record as a pertinent text on which to close. Here it is:

> Walter L. Gordon, chairman of the Royal Commission on Canada's Economic Prospects, told the Canadian Club of Toronto that Canadians 25 years from now may live in an era of conformity, doing and seeing the same things, driving the same kind of cars, living in the same kind of houses and thinking the same kind of thoughts. He could not see the times producing a reassuring crop of critics and debunkers and people who are independent and individualistic in their thinking and in their approach to life. "It is hard to see," he concluded, "where they are to come from in this comfortable, complacent and conforming age."

Is it too sanguine to hope that the verses collected in *The Blasted Pine* may be admitted as evidence that the non-conformist, individual spirit has never been without its manifestations in Canada, and that in the future the stubborn, subversive, intelligent reaction to the standardized life will continue to find a voice—at least from our poets and artists?

Will anyone listen?

TO JAY MACPHERSON
ON HER BOOK OF POEMS

1958

Dear no-man's-nightingale, our Fisher Queen,
Whose golden hook makes muddy waters green,
With what dexterity of wrist and eye
You flick the willow-rod and cast the fly:
And when the silver fish is caught and drawn,
How neat the table he's divided on,
How white the cloth, how elegant the dish,
How sweet the flesh—O sacramental Fish!

# A Garland
# For E. J. Pratt

## 1958

### THE POET

One of the distinguishing marks of a major poet is that his work continues, changes, develops, and increases in strength and vitality as he grows older. It has magnitude and volume as well as depth and quality, and it progressively demonstrates itself to be the fruit of experience and knowledge rather than of innocence and intuition. From the publication thirty-five years ago of the first of his seventeen volumes of poetry, Pratt's development has been consistent and sure. From the sea lyrics and personal impressions of *Newfoundland Verse* to the great heroic narratives, *The Roosevelt and the Antinoë* and *The Titanic*; from the Bacchanalian revelry of *The Witches' Brew* through the geophysical fantasias of *The Cachalot* and *The Great Feud* to the more explicit parable of *The Fable of the Goats* and the popular war poems, *Dunkirk* and *Behind the Log*; and from the religio-philosophical odes, *The Iron Door* and *The Truant*, to the grand conclusion of *Brébeuf and his Brethren*, the mastery in whatever field of poetry grew steadily more certain. In Pratt's poems of fantasy and imagination the theme is energy and dynamic action; in *The Titanic* and *Brébeuf*, his specifically human epics, the stage is at once narrower and more exalted, for the protagonist is man and the action is heroic. In his most recent poem, *Towards the Last Spike*, a verse-panorama of the building of the Canadian Pacific Railway, he combines fantasy and realism and introduces a new irony and a more mordant wit into his treatment of a theme that has engaged his interest from the beginning of his career: man's Promethean struggle with the blind forces of nature.

It is clear that Pratt has been an ambitious and serious poet, though never a solemn or dull one. In some ways he has been one of the most fortunate of poets. He has been honoured in his homeland and has succeded in pleasing reviewers and the general public as well as the literary critics, both of the academic sort and those that might be considered 'new'. And he seems to have done this without ever ceasing to please himself or, to put it another way, to do as he pleases. What he pleases to do has always been sparked by an immense gusto, but it has also always been controlled and directed by a strong sense of responsibility— primarily to himself—that is both aesthetic and if not religious at least moral. Ned Pratt is a modest man, but it is well that critics and expositors have not felt it necessary to make half-hearted claims for his poetry. On the whole they have done a solid, worth-while job. One thinks of the fine appraisals in W. E. Collins's *The White Savannahs* and in E. K. Brown's *On Canadian Poetry*, of the ambitious study by Henry W. Wells and Carl F. Klinck, of the glowing Introduction to Pratt's *Collected Poems* by William Rose Benét, and perhaps most significant of all, the late John Sutherland's 'new interpretation', which stresses the grandeur of the poet's reading of man's destiny.

Sutherland's essay is concerned with correcting what he believed to be some mistaken or incomplete ideas about the nature of the heroic in Pratt's poetry. Most critics have recognized that the idea of Power is fundamental in the poetry of Pratt, but it was left to Sutherland to analyse more exactly the moral and emotional attitudes that condition the poetry and that rise out of it. He points out that the poet's attitude towards Power is extremely complex and ambiguous, and that the emotions it arouses in him are complex and ambiguous also. These consist of exaltation and terror, and ultimately—this is where moral significance lies—compassion. These mixed emotions derive from the poet's ambiguous concept of power itself, which, Sutherland maintains, is a fusion of the Demoniac and the Heroic, the destroying force and the creative force. The important idea here is the idea of fusion, for Pratt's general philosophical theme is the resolution of conflict into harmony. Ambiguities are resolved dramatically into identities, and paradoxes exist to be resolved. The method most appropriate to this task is Irony. Irony gives Pratt's poetry its intellectual tang; what humanizes it and gives it its final calm is compassion.

This is difficult matter to put briefly. It will be clearer if I indicate how Sutherland applies his theory to one of Pratt's completest masterpieces, *The Titanic*, with its two sharply contrasted symbolic antagonists, the ship and the iceberg. 'The typical Pratt narrative', the critic wrote, 'is set upon the sea . . . its story and its symbolism often seems at cross-purposes; the story describes a conflict between human and natural power, man and sea, "hero" and "demon"—a conflict which is in part illusory, for the symbolism reveals their submerged likeness and tends to effect a fusion of the two protagonists.' And again: 'The ship and the iceberg may seem to represent at first the two poles of creative and destructive power, but the poem exists to prove they are almost identical symbols.'

Sutherland illuminates his argument with many illustrations drawn not only from *The Titanic* but from the two earlier fantasies, *The Great Feud* and *The Cachalot*. It might be demonstrated that the same fanaticism, the same stoical endurance and courage, the same devotion (but not to the same thing or from the same motive) exist in the 'demoniacal' Iroquois and the heroic Jesuits of *Brébeuf and His Brethren*. Here the significance lies in the distinction, in the unique source of the Ignatian heroism:

> the sound of invisible trumpets blowing
> Around two slabs of board, right-angled, hammered
> By Roman nails and hung on a Jewish hill. . . .

The identification remains on the purely human level; the difference is in the sphere of the divine. A better illustration of Sutherland's paradox is found in the other purely Canadian narrative, the entirely secular and very high-spirited *Towards the Last Spike*. Here, as in *The Titanic* and *The Roosevelt and the Antinoë*, the ostensible theme is a conflict between man and nature, between the creative force of man's will and this time not the ocean but the frozen rocky sea whose waves move only in the vast ages of geologic time, the Rocky Mountains and the Laurentian Shield. It is a conflict between the stony skeleton and the jagged protuberances of the continent itself and the little band of rock-like men, Macdonald, Stephen, Smith, Fleming, and Van Horne. Ironically—and this time happily, not tragically—the conflict is resolved because the human protagonists have the hardness, the endurance, and the flinty steadfastness of their rock-ribbed antagonist. Here is the figure of the antagonist as the Laurentian Shield (later it is to appear in the formidable guise of the Rocky Mountains):

> On the North Shore a reptile lay asleep—
> A hybrid that the myths might have conceived,
> But not delivered, as progenitor
> Of crawling, gliding things upon the earth.
> She lay snug in the folds of a huge boa
> Whose tail had covered Labrador and swished
> Atlantic tides, whose body coiled itself
> Around the Hudson Bay, then curled up north
> Through Manitoba and Saskatchewan
> To Great Slave Lake. In continental reach
> The neck went past the Great Bear Lake until
> Its head was hidden in the Arctic Seas.

We remember Sutherland's words about the ship and the iceberg and the conflict, 'in part illusory', between two protagonists whose submerged likeness tends to effect a fusion, for the railway builders who attack the Shield and the Mountains conquer because they take into themselves the strength and the power they are pitted against. These mountain men. And they are Scots. It is almost all summed up in that; but Pratt elaborates, and his elaboration, while it bears out much that John Sutherland has discerned, illustrates also an essential quality of Pratt's art that Sutherland somewhat characteristically tended to ignore—the quality of humour. Here is how the poet sees them:

> Oatmeal was in their blood and in their names.
> Thrift was the title of their catechism.
> It governed all things but their mess of porridge
> Which, when it struck the hydrochloric acid
> With treacle and skim-milk, became a mash.
> Entering the duodenum, it broke up
> Into amino acids: then the liver
> Took on its natural job as carpenter:
> Foreheads grew into cliffs, jaws into juts.
> The meal so changed, engaged the follicles:
> Eyebrows came out as gorse, the beards as thistles,
> And the chest-hair the fell of Grampian rams.
> It stretched and vulcanized the human span:
> Nonagenerations worked and thrived on it.
> Out of such chemistry run through by genes,
> The food released its fearsome racial products:—
> The power to strike a bargain like a foe,
> To win an argument upon a burr,
> Invest the language with a Bannockburn,
> Culloden or the warnings of Lochiel. . . .

This is humorous and at times witty imaginative description. Metaphorically it is both surprising and just. Hyperbole is made to seem literal, and the ordinary is made surprising. There is the combination of unexpected and remotely-gathered perceptions that we associate with the metaphysical conceit, and the whole passage seems to me to illustrate the unity of sensibility that Mr. Eliot has declared to be characteristic of seventeenth-century poetry and of little poetry since.

Yet these qualities, though they are perhaps more abundantly displayed in Pratt's last poem, are found in his earliest, in some of his Newfoundland verses and shorter lyrics of the thirties. In one of these, *The Stoics*, which begins

They were the oaks and beeches of our species.
Their roots struck down through acid loam
To weathered granite and took hold
Of flint and silica,

there is a curious anticipation of the passage about the railway builders. It is an interesting exercise in practical criticism to analyse the development of a method and see a style in the act of perfecting itself. This is in little what we can do on a larger scale if we read through Pratt's works in their chronological order. To do so is to realize that one of the distinguishing marks of a major poet is that his work continues, changes, develops, and increases in strength as he grows older.

# TWO BOOK REVIEWS

(i) STANZAS WRITTEN
ON FIRST LOOKING
INTO JOHNSTON'S *AUK**
1959

Mrs bloody Bikini Balls
　　My cousin thrice removed
In the paddy van to the vasty halls
　　Of the mad and the mis-beloved
Capers and jiggles and sings like hell
(And Mrs Beleek belike as well).

A little bit tight alright alright
　　She carols a cracked old song
Of a dreamland bright she can reach at night
　　By a trail that is winding and long.
And Mrs Beleek belike as well
Joins in the song for of it the hell.

Like a couple of mad Bacchantes they
　　Cut off poor Edward's nuts
(He owed me a fiver I'm sorry to say)
　　And refusing to hear any *Ifs* or *Buts*
Read Frye on *The Marriage of Heaven and Hell*
And eke on Mrs Beleek as well.

My cousin Balls (AND my Auntie Crap!)
　　Are a little bit cracked but loads of fun.
And I myself am a whimsical chap,
　　A Betjeman manqué, if not a Donne,
Who dwells in a suburban sort of a hell
With Mrs Beleek belike as well.

* George Johnston, *The Cruising Auk*, 1959.

## (ii) THE DEVIL TAKE HER — AND THEM
### 1962

I left the woman spread like jam on the bed.
I roared like a stricken pig or a pride
Of lions. I scrammed. No humpety ride
To Paradise tonight, you bitch, I cried.
I said if you still had your maidenhead
You could keep it still for all of me. I'd
Rather try for a hole in one, I lied,
Or take a copy of *Playboy* into bed.

What had she done to bring this tantrum on?
The same as she'd done for a couple of weeks.
Ever since reading *Love Where the Nights are Long**
She had kept on turning her other cheeks
And sighing for all the lyrical feats
Of poets in Montreal between the sheets.

* Edited by Irving Layton, 1962.

# The Poet and the Nuclear Crisis

## 1965

These are times that try men's souls.

I mean this literally. Not in the sense that men's souls are irked, annoyed, or exasperated, but that they are tested and brought to judgement.

And this judgement is so deadly that if we fail or are found wanting, civilization, if not the race itself, faces annihilation—drawn up, like Marlowe's Dr. Faustus "Into the entrails of yon labouring cloud," and like Faustus also, unable to find a foolproof shelter:

> Then will I headlong run into the earth.
> Earth gape! O, no, it will not harbour me!

One almost feels that the description of Faustus' last hour is a prophecy of the fate of Faustian man, the Renaissance universal man, approaching his tragic climax in our own age.

Professor Arnold Toynbee only last year described the nature of our plight in words that deserve to be remembered.

> The year 1949 opened a new era in human history. Before that date the survival of the human race had been assured ever since the time, part way through the Paleolithic age, when mankind had won a decisive and unchallengeable ascendancy over all other forms of life on this planet as well as over inanimate nature. Between that time and the year 1949 man's crimes and follies could and did wreck civilizations and bring unnecessary and undeserved sufferings upon countless numbers of men, women, and children. But the worst that man could do with his pre-atomic technology was not enough to enable him to destroy his own race. Genocide, at least, was beyond his power until the atomic weapon had been invented and had been acquired by more states than one. . . .

The tragic thing is that this fatal technological skill, which demands that man exert an almost superhuman moral self-control, has been acquired at the very moment when there has been, if not a breakdown, certainly a weakening of religious and ethical sanctions.

The scientist, the statesman, and the soldier seem to have failed us. I suggest that we must turn to the scholar, the historian, the philosopher, and above all to the poet, who in his capacity as prophetic interpreter of the imagination may even become a saviour.

The peculiar responsibility of the poet in this age of anxiety and fear is to awaken the imagination and touch the conscience of humanity. I say *humanity* because this is a work in which Frost and Pasternak are not rivals but collaborators.

What are some of the qualities or properties of poetry that make it a fit instrument for registering (and affecting) the imaginative intuition and the ethical spirit of our time?

The qualities we seek must be such as will sharpen our perception of reality and intensify our sense of what it means to be a human being. Can poetry help us, in the apt phrase of Stringfellow Barr, to re-join the human race?

I believe it can.

Poetry has both a personal and a communal use. It draws mankind together by extending the power of feeling, while at the same time it sharpens and intensifies it. Poetry is an instrument of self-awareness, and awareness, and like charity, begins at home. Without it we cannot usefully take up the burden of politics and ethics.

The late R. G. Collingwood, the English philosopher and historian, in *The Principles of Art*, called poetry "the community's medicine for the worst disease of the mind, the corruption of consciousness." Because of its medicinal, therapeutic, and cathartic function, poetry must often seem distasteful. If I may repeat here what I said at the Kingston Conference, later published in *Writing in Canada*, "Poetry is language and feeling purified of the superficial. All the smooth, polite, gentle compromises that make for easiness and good humour in a suburban society, poetry brushes aside or ignores or penetrates beneath." Either directly or by implication it is critical and impatient.

This is true not only of a Ginsberg, a Ferlinghetti, or an Irving Layton but of Catullus, Ovid, Dante, Donne, Blake, Baudelaire —of all the greatest poets. And of Swift, for all poets do not write in verse. By poetry I mean here imaginative and prophetic writing in whatever mode or form. Let me claim Swift as a poet, at least in his greatest work, and use him to illustrate my thesis.

The great Dean of St. Patrick's, whose heart, as his self-composed epitaph tells us, was lacerated with savage indignation, has written in the second and fourth books of *Gulliver's Travels* some passages that since 1949 have taken on an intensity and relevance that even the dark mind of Swift could not have imagined.

Dr. Lemuel Gulliver, that typical patriotic well-meaning English medical man of the Whig ascendancy, is offering to communicate the modern European scientific know-how in the art of war to the humane and enlightened monarch of Brobdignag:

> In hopes to ingratiate myself farther into his Majesty's favour, I told him of an invention, discovered between three and four hundred years ago, to make a certain powder, into an heap of which the smallest spark of fire falling, would kindle the whole in a moment, . . . and make it all fly up in the air together, with a noise and agitation greater than thunder.

The good man of science goes on to describe the manufacture and use of cannon-balls, shells, cannon, mortars, and mines. He outlines the devastation that these instruments wreak upon fortifications, walls, towns, ships, and human bodies; and speaks of the irresistible power that the possession of such weapons would confer on the King, both for the purpose of keeping his own people subservient and of conquering his neighbour's dominions.

But what does the King reply?

> The King was struck with horror at the description I had given of the terrible engines, and the proposal I had made. He was amazed, how so impotent and grovelling an insect as I . . . could entertain such inhuman ideas, and in so familiar a manner as to appear wholly unmoved at all the scenes of blood and desolation, which I had painted as the common effects of those destructive machines; whereof he said some evil genius, enemy to mankind, must have been the first contriver.

"A strange effect," comments Gulliver (like our own exponents of arms races and testings), "of narrow principles and short views!"

By how many megatons must we multiply the weight of this denunciation to make it adequate to the situation as we know it today?

In our own age, more certainly than in Swift's, the name of the Muse, alas, is Cassandra. "I will show you fear in a handful of dust," she speaks in the voice of Mr. Eliot; or cries in W. B. Yeats's "The Second Coming":

> Things fall apart; the centre cannot hold;
> Mere anarchy is loosed upon the world,
> The blood-dimmed tide is loosed, and everywhere
> The ereemony of innocence is drowned . . .

or warns us in Auden's "For The Time Being":

> The evil and armed draw near;
> The weather smells of their hate
> And the houses smell of our fear.
> Death has opened his white eye . . .

These are the voices of the poet in our time. Let us listen for a moment to the voice of a scientist—but a scientist who is also a novelist, the English writer, Sir Charles Snow. During the war, Snow worked alongside the men in England who were contributing their scientific skill to the development of the bomb that was later to be dropped on Hiroshima and Nagasaki, and he described their actions and reactions and their responses to what was done in his novel, *The New Men*. His own point of view has been stated concisely in a number of reviews and critical articles. I will quote a short passage from one of these that appeared in the London *Spectator* in March 1954. Snow presents very vividly the moral dilemma in which the scientists found themselves. "Scientists have decided themselves [as to the true nature of the problem] less than most of us," he writes. "When the bombs were dropped the scientists I knew were even more horrified than the rest of us. Their horror was not simple; it contained the outrage of conscience, but it also contained an edge of fear." The outrage of conscience, however, was the more intense feeling.

> The release of atomic energy was the greatest single triumph of applied science: applied science had, even despite total wars, done far more good than harm to man's material existence: but now the first use of its greatest triumph was to bring about the largest slaughter of any day in human history.

Something of what this involved had been mentioned earlier in the article: "With each bomb a population about the size of Oxford was destroyed, men, women, and children: the lucky were burned to death, or blasted to death, in a matter of instants: the others lingered."

Sir Charles finds a somewhat uncertain hope that mutual fear on the part of the Soviet Union and the United States will be strong enough to prevent a future disaster:

But I also believe that moral forces have not been quite negligible. I believe that the horror which most men felt when the two bombs were dropped, the horror which left on so many scientists a moral scar, has had an effect which is small by the scale of world events but neither altogether contemptible nor altogether selfish. It think it possible that a good many men, certainly in the West and maybe elsewhere, have asked themselves a question—for what purposes are we justified in doing these things to other men?

To contemplate and prepare for (in the name of defence) the instantaneous destruction of millions of human beings suggests a failure in the realm of morals and religion that is certainly a much more complete breakdown than anything testified to by teen-age delinquency or isolated individual violence or crime. And when this possibility is accepted with equanimity by a society and culture that believes (or professes to believe) that God is Love, holds that the Sermon on the Mount is the noblest expression of practical morality, and venerates Socrates and Jesus as our highest teachers, we are in the presence of an irony that might be tragic if it weren't so pitiful, and that cries out for a poet as powerful as Dante or a satirist as bitter as Swift to express it.

A moral shudder ought to be sweeping the world; but there has been a failure of the imagination: we seem powerless to fear enough what may be done to us or to abhor enough what we contemplate doing to others.

It is in both these realms—that of imagination and that of morality—that the poet and artist, even more certainly than the philosopher, the theologian, and the *good* scientist, can play his part.

Poetry alone is perhaps unequal to the magnitude of the task. Only religion—but not religion alone, religion finding its voice in poetry—can unite humanism and moral fervour and provide an instrument and a technic that may be adequate to the task.

Certain poets of the twentieth century—T. S. Eliot, Edith Sitwell, W. H. Auden, and Dylan Thomas, to name only those who come first to mind—have become religious poets under the pressure of the destructive forces unleashed in this age of the great wars. They have shown us in some of their best poems what the reaction of the human heart must be in the face of an almost superhuman yet man-made evil.

Eliot, Sitwell, and Thomas (and they are not alone, of course) lived through the London blitz of 1940. They were faced with a lesser horror than we are today—had we the imagination and conviction to feel it—but they experienced this earlier baptism of fire in its immediacy and (being poets) with all their senses and all their mind. When one reads such intensely felt poems as Edith Sitwell's "Still Falls the Rain," Eliot's "Little Gidding" (the last and greatest of the *Four Quartets*), or Dylan Thomas's "Ceremony after a Fire Raid" or "A Refusal to Mourn the Death, by Fire, of a Child in London," we realise that ordinary realistic familiar poetry has been made obsolete. An apocalyptic, ritualistic, visionary, and sometimes mystical poetry alone is capable of dealing with this experience or of probing into its moral or spiritual significance.

Here is a part of the opening section of Dylan Thomas' "Ceremony after a Fire Raid":

Myselves
The grievers
Grieve
Among the street burned to tireless death
A child of a few hours
With its kneading mouth
Charred on the black breast of the grave
The mother dug, and its arms full of fires.

Begin
With singing
Sing
Darkness kindled back into the beginning
When the caught tongue nodded blind,
A star was broken
Into the centuries of the child
Myselves grieve now, and miracles cannot atone.

Forgive
Us forgive
Us your death that myselves the believers
May hold it in a great flood
Till the blood shall spurt,
And the dust shall sing like a bird
As the grains blow, as your death grows, through our heart.

One can hardly fail to notice here how unmistakably, if only by implication, the dead infant is identified with Christ—("A star was broken/Into the centuries of the child")—and how the guilt must be accepted by all of us, the child's fellow citizens, and does not belong only to the immediate agents of his death. But the poem needs a thoughtful reading if we are to discover (through the references to the blood that shall spurt and the grains that shall blow through our heart) that it is the celebration of an expiatory mass.

Another poem on the raids of 1940 which like this achieves a marrage of poetry and religion is Edith Sitwell's "Still Falls the Rain." In this, horror and pity are fused with a devotional intensity that suggests medieval Christian art. Of the four elements, earth, air, fire, and water, it is fire, the rain of fire, that dominates the poem and the whole tragedy of Faustian man rises from his rejection of Christ and the endless wounding of his body by the cruelty and pride of our wars. At the climax of the poem the rain of fire descending from the bombers is equated with the blood of Christ. The identification of sinful man, victim and aggressor alike, with Faust is made explicit by a quotation from the tremendous final scene of Marlowe's *Dr. Faustus*, where the flames of hell leap up to engulf Faust, who calls upon Christ too late:

> Still falls the Rain—
> Then—O Ile leape ûp to my God: who pulls me doune—
>   See, see where Christ's blood streames in the firmament:
>   It flows from the Brow we nailed upon the tree
> Deep to the dying, to the thirsting heart
> That holds the fires of the world,—dark-smirched with pain
> As Caesar's laurel crown.
>
> Then sounds the voice of One who like the heart of man
> Was once a child who among beasts has lain—
> 'Still do I love, still shed my innocent light, my Blood, for thee.'

With the invention of the nuclear bomb and the two tragic occasions of its actual use in war, the moral and religious tension expressed in Edith Sitwell's poems of 1940 increased almost beyond endurance.

In 1952 Penguin Books published a widely circulated selection of her poems. The place of honour at the beginning of the book was reserved for what she named "Three Poems for the Atomic Age." These were "Dirge for the New Sunrise," "The Shadow of Cain," and "The Canticle of the Rose." Their theme is again the guilt we all share—as Christians and as human beings—and the power of the feeling they generate approaches a sort of controlled hysteria. The beginning and end of the "Dirge for the New Sunrise" will indicate something of the apocalyptic power and moral fervour with which this poetry assumes the responsibility of registering the shock to the conscience of the world:

> Bound to my heart as Ixion to the wheel,
> Nailed to my heart as the thief upon the cross,
> I hang between our Christ and the gap where the world was
>     lost
>
> And watch the phantom Sun in Famine Street—
> The ghost of the heart of Man . . . red Cain,
> But I saw the little Ant-men as they ran
> Carrying the world's weight of the world's filth
> And the filth in the heart of Man—
> Compressed till those lusts and greeds had a greater heat
> than that of the Sun.
> And the ray from the heat came soundless, shook the sky
> As if in search for food, and squeezed the stems
> Of all that grows on the earth till they were dry.
> —And drank the marrow of the bone:
> The eyes that saw, the lips that kissed, are gone,
> Or black as thunder lie and grin at the murdered Sun.
>
> The living blind and seeing dead together lie
> As if in love. . . . There was no more hating then—
> And no more love: Gone is the heart of Man.

As a poet, I myself can testify to the overbearing pressure of this crisis of the heart, a crisis of conscience that is compounded of fear and humiliation, a pressure that impinges upon us all, whether we are aware of it or not, with an ever increasing force. Gremlins jump out at us from the newspaper or TV screen, ogres coo or roar from every radio, and a sense of guilt assails us (not as Americans or Canadians or Russians or Frenchmen or Englishmen; not as Christians or Jews or Moslems; but simply as human beings, men and women, not cuckoos, apes, asses, donkeys, pigs or tigers)—the inescapable feeling of shame we experience when we hear certain names—Belsen, Guernica, Hiroshima, Budapest, Dresden.

I also have had to write on this subject. I will read now a sequence of three short poems written over the whole extended period of the Cold War. I read them not so much for their own sake as because they illustrate the theme of this paper.

The first poem in the series was written in 1946. It is called "Business as Usual", and it sums up—a little ironically perhaps—our American sense of being finished with the unwanted entanglements of war, and ready to get back with relief to minding our own business.

But of course this proved impossible, a premature and soon abandoned hope; and so when in 1954 I was collecting some poems to form a volume I realised that this piece was out-dated and untrue. It could not stand alone. I continued it therefore, or rather, wrote it over again in the light of what was happening then. We were testing atomic weapons in the Pacific and the nuclear arms race had begun. Some Japanese fishermen had been injured, and few of us—as Christians or simply as men of good will—were not very happy or satisfied. Also we were afraid. This second poem of the sequence, then, is called "Fear as Normal."

And now in 1962 when I was again getting ready some poems for a book I saw once more that the poem was outmoded and inadequate. The blast (of the poem, that is) was not in the megaton range: what had to be done, in a third and parallel poem, was to intensify the pressure. If the first two expressed scorn and pity, this one would have to heighten these emotions and resolutely reject any temptation to partiality or compromise. The only way was to withdraw to an almost astronomical distance—as Toynbee or Frazer do—so that the situation can be seen as involving the whole planet and all mankind. The last of the three poems is called—rather sadly and again ironically—"Universal Peace."

BUSINESS AS USUAL, 1946

Across the craggy indigo
Come rumours of the flashing spears,
And in the clank of rancid noon
There is a tone, and such a tone.
How tender! How insidious!
The air grows gentle with protecting bosks,
And furry leaves take branch and root.
Here we are safe, we say, and slyly smile.

In this delightful forest, fluted so,
We burghers of the sunny central plain
Fable a still refuge from the spears
That clank—but gently clank—but clank again!

## FEAR AS NORMAL, 1954

But gently clank? The clank has grown
A flashing crack—the crack of doom.
It mushrooms high above our salty plain,
and plants the sea with rabid fish.

How skilful! How efficient!
The active cloud is our clenched fist.
Hysteria, dropping like the gentle dew,
Over the bent world broods with ah! bright wings.

We guess it dazzles our black foe;
But that it penetrates and chars
Our own Christ-laden lead-encaséd hearts
Our terrified fierce dreamings know.

## UNIVERSAL PEACE, 19—

Murder and suicide alas
The double crime our pride commends.
Too much and much too soon
The stockpile overkill condones.

The boom that boomerangs
Around the sphere and what was twi-divided
Joins—how neat!—how dead!—
A pock-marked scorched colossal Moon.

Hatred and Fear: twins locked in a dead womb.
Blind ice in orbit: heart and head
Burned, cooled, cold, killed—
*Pax mundi* singed and signed and sealed.

Let me add a brief note on two passages in these poems.
The sentence

Hysteria dropping like the gentle dew,
Over the bent world broods with ah! bright wings

quotes ironically two famous passages, one by Shakespeare and the other by Gerard Manly Hopkins. In Portia's speech, of course, it is "the quality of mercy" which "droppeth like the gentle dew from heaven"; and in Hopkins' sonnet "God's Grandeur" it is the Holy Ghost which "over the bent world broods with warm breast and with ah! bright wings." Today, it is neither man's mercy nor the grandeur of the Holy Ghost, but the mushroom cloud that broods over the bent (that is, the twisted, perverted) world.

The other note is on the line "The stockpile overkill condones," and it is just a brief statistical corroboration. I quote from the study by Harrison Brown and James Real, *The Community of Fear:* "It is estimated that the U.S. and the U.S.S.R. together possess explosive material corresponding to about sixty billion tons of TNT or about twenty tons of TNT for every inhabitant of the world."

The irony is in the fact.

But irony and the poetry of irony are not enough. Irony, satire, and even invective are fine, but they are largely negative. Despair, like apathy, is criminal.

Where our salvation lies is hard to see—though where it certainly does not lie is plain. It does not lie in indifference or acquiescence; above all it does not lie in continuing the arms race and in spreading the possession of nuclear weapons to an ever larger collection of states. Our poets know this well enough; and they know too, more profoundly, I think, than most of us, that the nuclear threat is a denial of life at its essential source. The young Canadian poet Milton Acorn in his poem "On the Toronto Fall-out Shelter," published in his recent volume *Jawbreakers*, is obsessed with the horror of a shadow that corrupts the very nucleus of life itself, sex, which is the beginning and continuation of life. To contemplate the killing of others on a grand scale is to kill the self, to kill one's own self. There is no defence and no escape. It is an integration of suicide, and to huddle in communal shelters is to return to a pre-natal and sterile womb.

Knowing this, we ask for something positive. Poet and philosopher-historian alike suggest our salvation will be found (if at all) where Jesus and Socrates said it would.

In "September 1, 1939", written at the beginning of the Second World War, W. H. Auden put our case and suggested a remedy:

> Defenceless under the night
> Our world in stupor lies;
> Yet dotted everywhere,
> Ironic points of light
> Flash out wherever the Just
> Exchange their messages.

And the messages are simply this:

We must love one another or die.

A hard thing to do, you say, and I agree. But we must make the attempt: we have no choice. Arnold Toynbee has put it like this: "The negative deterrent provided by mutual fear would have to be replaced by the positive bond of mutual love if the human race was to regain the certitude of survival." Another great English publicist and historian, A. J. P. Taylor, reviewing a number of books on the strategy of nuclear warfare in the *New Statesman*, recently agreed with the poets that the problem, is essentially an ethical and religious one. "All these books," he wrote, "are to me a buzzing in the ears.... They all ask 'How can I prevent nuclear weapons being dropped on me?' This seems to me the wrong question. The right one is: 'Would I drop these weapons on others in any circumstances?'"

This is indeed a difficult forebearance that is asked of us— almost as difficult, indeed, as to be a Christian, a Platonist, or a humanist. But it is the arts and the humanities, and particularly poetry, the most humane of all the arts, that can offer that education in sensibility and virtue that we must submit to if we are to live.

## POET IN RESIDENCE, BISHOP'S UNIVERSITY
(for Ralph Gustafson)
1965

Our Ralph? A poet is he? Walks he here
Among us studious ants in Academe?
—Head lifted, locks uncumbered, halo tipt
A trifle rakish, though invisible,
And goatsfoot sheathed in gleaming Cordovan?
Behold! Our Bishop's nourishes a bard
Again.
        Where Drummond mimicked *joual*
And Scott, not yet canonical, drank deep
Of the Pierian spring, as did his son,
As did McCrae, who sleeps where poppies blow,
He sings.
          Lived has he? Suffered has he? Toiled
To ply the homely slighted shepherd's trade?
—We can but guess.
             Yet sure, his lyre's in tune
(His portable Corona, fact puts in)
And follows faithful wheresoe'er he goes,
Be it Vienna, Knossos, Revelstoke,
Vadstena, or Milan's cathedral's roof,
And pours song forth (though often gnarled with
      thought
And knotty syntax too) as crystalline
In Salzburg or Bayreuth as by the blue
Cold lakes that bathe the base of icy crags
And peaks Canadian that dare a man
To scale Parnassus.
           How came he poet?
Who shall say? Yet read his verses as they're writ
—Not with mind's calculating eye alone
But with the heart's, and then the secret's out,
The secret many a cryptic poem shouts
—An *ars poetica* in two small words:
                    *my love!*

TO FRANK SCOTT; ESQ.
On the Occasion of his Seventieth Birthday
1969

Poet and Man of Law—O brave anomaly!—
dove wise and serpent-tongued for Song or Plea—
a parti-colored animal, committed, *parti-pris*
but not a party man, a Man, and free.

Padlock unlocker and voice with a key,
unbanner of books, and by a natural necessity
against duplicity and privileged Duplessisy.

But what endears you most to me,
old friend, 's your love and practice of sweet poesy.

I ask, then, what it means to be a poet:
—to grasp the Muse's saxophone and blow it?
—to have a quivering soul, and show it?

—to prance in purple like an Emperor's clown?
or tickle the gallant salons of the town?
or lift the Holy Grail, and toss it down?

Not today, I think. Wrong answers drop,
facile as angels' tears, and plop
so dully unctuous you cry, "For God's sake, STOP!"

To be a poet, Frank, you've shown
's a harder thing. It is to be a stone,
an eye, a heart, a lung, a microphone,

a voice, but not a voice alone, a hand,
a hand to grasp a hand, a leg to stand
on, nerves to feel, and in supreme command

the shaping mind that shapes the poem
as it shapes the man, foursquare, and needle-eyed,
and Frank.

# The Poetics of
# Alfred G. Bailey

## 1974

Next to Margaret Avison, Alfred Bailey is probably the most difficult and sometimes obscure poet writing in Canada today and during the last three decades, and like her he is one of the most original, significant, and genuinely rewarding. In his poetry quite as much as in his scholarly essays collected in *Culture and Nationality* and his contributions to *A Literary History of Canada*, Alfred Bailey is an historian, an anthoropologist, and an adventurous explorer of new ways of enriching the language of metaphor. This last, of course, is a characteristic of his activity as a poet, but it is used to bring the subjects of his poetry and his prose closer together. As well as being an original and an experimental poet, Bailey is a scholarly, learned, and traditional poet. His work is squarely centered in the modern metaphysical line to which each in his own way Hopkins, Eliot, Hart Crane, and Empson belong. "Each in his own way" is important, and Alfred Bailey has his own way, too.

Just what that is and how it differs from those of the poets named is difficult to put into words or describe briefly, but perhaps by citing relevant passages I can do it. It will be fun to try, anyhow.

First a few generalizations may be helpful. The general subject of many of the most exciting poems in this book*is history—fairly local with respect to place (New Brunswick mainly but the Eastern seaboard also, including occasionally also New England and Virginia) but going back in time as far as the French-English-Indian wars of the seventeenth and eighteenth centuries and farther still to the Algonkian culture before the coming of the white man. A few of these poems I have admired for years—"Border River", "Algonkian Burial", "Miramichi Lightning", "Ideogram", and "Colonial Set", to name only a few—but others, especially in the first and fourth sections are new, or new to me.

Among the unfamiliar pieces, especially in the first section of

---

* *Thanks for a Drowned Island.* By A. G. Bailey, Toronto: McClelland & Stewart Ltd., 1973.

the book, are some that develop Bailey's technical innovations more fully than any of the nevertheless very original poems I have named. These are poems not of history but of nature (animals and weather, sea and earth) and of men and machines (tramp steamers, docks, steam shovels), and their skill and effectiveness depend on the unexpected metaphors, resulting often in conceits, the surprising pertinence of implication, and what seems like an unexpected bonus of 'music' in the peppering of rhyme, alliteration, and assonance providing an appropriately tough accompaniment to the thought and feeling.

But perhaps only some examples can make these observations valid. Near the beginning of the book we come upon a poem entitled "how in the dark our index page to find"—a title that puts the reader on his mettle its relevance to find, an absorbing but not an impossible task. The unifying central image (or symbol?) is the column of black smoke pouring from the stack of a tramp steamer coming into dock in a heavy sea. I will have to quote the poem in its entirety.

        dock take ship trundling
        bundled in funnel's
        smoke; devil take
        sea chop and oil slick.
        Break
        all foul mix,
        sea-lung gone
        from green bayed edges
        to black grampus fix. The
        sea's eyes would
        green wind, send
        and shiver tramps and
        good-hulled traders.
        See if wind steps up
        snarling dogs of
        water lumps, dumping all
        craft over,
        (hail, hail careless sea) and
        careless empty rover
        and cracks clanging bells. Sea
        smells point noses ammonia sharp;
        bells make hark, hear
        (meaning see)
        the ghost
        of holy and
        rewarded smoke,

for good and vertical
virtues find
their blooming goal
and hope, the most.

Here the poet's impeccable ear modulates the rhythms through the varying line lengths and the distribution of the breaks required by the sense, and the resulting harsh and grating 'music' contributes almost as much as the images to the communication of 'meaning'. It testifies also the genuineness of the emotion. What emotion? You ask.

Why, the pleasure and indeed the thrill of recognizing in a common and maybe commonplace event—certainly an 'unpoetic' one—and instance of man's hard, necessary, and here successful struggle with nature (in this case sea and wind) so that the dirty black smoke pouring from the tramp steamer's funnel becomes ghostly, holy, and rewarding—sacred as the smoke of a thank offering on the altar of a temple. The clanging bells on bridge and in engine room are a celebration of the elevation of a host.

And now the title. The poem itself we see illustrates how in the dark of humdrum dangerous ordinary work the mind that imaginatively sees connections can find direction and guidance to the place of meanings.

And that is perhaps what all the poems in this book—even the most difficult—achieve. And so too do some of the simpler delightful nature poems, which are not about any of the grand or grandiose or picturesque aspects of scenery but about the humbler flowers and animals—dandelions, muskrats, moles,—such poems for example as "Water, Air, Fire, Earth", "The Muskrat and the Whale", or "The Sun the Wind the Summer Field".

The paradoxical celebration of the muskrat at the expense of the mighty whale is an almost perfect Marianne Moore poem (I mean this as praise)—but there is a difference. Once again I must quote:

The muskrat in his book is
    not a contemptible fellow. . . .
His reason
liberates his nights and days in
the medium this reason both foreshadows
                and reflects.
He is satisfied and we are satisifed to
                see him so.
We would not want his goings-out and
                comings-in,
deliberate and slow, . . .

Dignity and industry lend size to the muskrat.
His size is his own, and mete.
The whale may think his dignity is greater.
The muskrat would be able, if the
                              thought struck him,
to prove his own title to this quality,
                              sooner or later.

This has the charm and delight of Marianne Moore's quixotic observations, but the difference is that not only the frogs (muskrats) are real but the gardens ("the shallow bed of gurgling water he works and plays in") are not imaginary but real.

Such poems as those I have been considering I find more pleasing—perhaps because they are 'purer' poetry—than the set pieces on Canadian history, such as "The Shadow of Mr. McGee", "Canadian Flag Debate", and "Confederation Debate", though heaven knows these are witty, clever, and perceptive enough to enliven subjects that journalists and text-books have made dull. Here for once we have a Canadian poet writing as well as our historians—perhaps because this poet is an historian too.

In conclusion I should say that this book once again demonstrates the continuing vitality of the intellectual tradition in Canadian poetry and places Alfred Bailey in the forefront of a significant group of poets that includes F. R. Scott, Eli Mandel, Ralph Gustafson, Douglas LePan, and a few others. Of none of these can it be said that in their poetry there is "so little for the mind".

# The Confessions of a Compulsive Anthologist

## 1976

As early as my first high school days I was everlastingly making lists—lists of favorite books, of favorite poems, which soon developed into lists of the 'best' books, the 'best' poems—or rather, what in my slowly diminishing ignorance I thought at the time were the 'best'. My parents accused me of always having my nose in a book, and it is true that I used to read one of our English texts, *Poems of the Romantic Revival*, under my desk at school during some of the duller classes such as Geography or Latin. At home I read the exciting adventure serials in *Chums* or *The Boy's Own Annual*, to be followed soon by Stevenson and even Scott. It wasn't hard to notice that the writing in *Kidnapped* or *Treasure Island* was lighter, swifter, and more vivid than in *Ivanhoe* or *The Talisman*. So was the action, and so, I think, though I could not have put a name to it then, was the quality of the imagination. Taste was developing (in poetry too), but any principles upon which it could be based were unknown, and unconsciously taken for granted. I saw nothing ridiculous in Palgrave's astonishing attempt, as he confessed it in the Introduction to *The Golden Treasury*, "to include ... all the best original Lyrical pieces and Songs in our language ... by writers not living—and none beside the best." I liked many of the poems, especially those from the Elizabethan Age and the Seventeenth Century, and, of course Keats and Shelley.

In Westmount High and at McGill in the twenties no modern poetry (except Kipling) was taught—and little Canadian poetry (except Carman). Indeed, one of my high school teachers seeing me with a copy of Masefield's *Ballads and Poems* said, "That's rather strong stuff, isn't it?" I had to discover modern poetry for myself—more or less by chance. In the Westmount Public Library I came upon *The New Poetry* edited by Harriet Monroe and Alice Corbin Henderson, published in 1917. And here I read with delight and fascination the new poetry of Ezra Pound, Wallace Stevens, T. S. Eliot, Yeats in his middle period, Conrad Aiken, and H. D. This, I think is a complete list of the poets whom I deliberately began to imitate in the earliest apprentice verses I printed there or four years later in the *Literary Supplement* to the *McGill Daily* and the *McGill Fortnightly Review.* These mostly appeared under various romantic pseudonyms. Vincent Starr, Simeon Lamb and Michael Gard are some I remember. Brian Tuke and Bernard March were Frank Scott.

At that time — 1923-24 — I had read no Canadian poetry except Carman's *Pipes of Pan* series and *Sappho* and was not encouraged to read any by what I found in Wilfred Campbell's *Oxford Book of Canadian Verse* of 1913 or Garvin's *Canadian Poets* (complete with photographs) of 1916. During the twenties when F.R.S. and I were at McGill there seemed to be no Canadian poetry that was new, intelligent and contemporary and no magazine or journal that would publish such poetry were it to appear. For myself, I determined to study and practice, and to test the value of any piece by submitting it to the best English or American literary magazines — and to the *Canadian Forum*, the one exception I should have noted above, a journal which from its inception in 1920 until today has championed the cause of modernism both in poetry and criticism. While still at the university I counted myself fortunate to have poems accepted by the *Forum* and by Mark Van Doren for the *Nation* and by Marianne Moore for *The Dial.* I was pleased to find in *The Dial* some poems by another Canadian, W. W. E. Ross, about whom I knew nothing; and in Ezra Pound's little magazine, *Exile,* and the Parisian *avant garde* magazine, *This Quarter,* stories by Morley Callaghan, of Toronto. At this time too Raymond Knister was publishing stories in the Iowa magazine *The Midland* and poems in the *Canadian Forum* and, I think, *This Quarter,* in which an early draft of part of John Glassco's *Memoirs of Montparnasse* also appeared. This was the beginning of modern literature in Canada, and it began in Paris and the U.S. as well as in Canada.

I suppose the first anthology of 'modern' poetry in Canada and the first I had anything to do with was *New Provinces* (1936). The original idea was Frank Scott's. It was to have been simply a selection of poems by four friends who had been contributors to the *McGill Fortnightly Review* (1924-25) and the *Canadian Mercury* (1928-29) — Frank Scott, Leo Kennedy, A. M. Klein, and myself. The selections were made by Frank and me, working in close collaboration as editors, making the final selection and more or less shaping the policy of the venture. We decided that we ought to broaden the scope of the book a bit, and we invited two Toronto poets, Robert Finch, whose elegant dandiacal poems I very much admired, and E. J. Pratt, the only one of us who had a reputation as a poet and was at all well known. I was away teaching in Indiana and then at Michigan State in the first two or three years of the thirties when the book was being prepared. I left the correspondence regarding the contents of the book to Frank. I was to write an Introduction. I gather from letters I saw many years later that our Toronto guests considered themselves equally editors and expressed their opinions frankly of all the accepted inclusions, which, of course, was all to the good—except, I hope I shall not be blamed for thinking, the rejection by Ned Pratt and the publisher, Hugh Eayres, of the Introduction I had written and mailed in to Scott. The objections to some of it were valid enough. Worse than the rejection of all Canadian poetry before ours—or at least that to be found in the anthologies of Garvin and Campbell—was the tone of rather youthful arrogance and perhaps the scornful epigrammatic style—faults (and virtues) to be found also in my 1928 *Canadian Forum* article, "Wanted—Canadian Criticism." I still think this attitude was needed in the middle thirties and would have had a salutary effect had it been published then. There was much also that was serious, as the concluding brief paragraph may indicate:

> That the poet is not a dreamer but a man of sense; that poetry is a discipline because it is an art; and that it is further a useful art: these are propositions which it is intended this volume shall suggest. We are not deceiving ourselves that it has proved them.

In the face of Pratt's threat to withdraw and Macmillan's not to publish, Scott had no choice but to withdraw the Introduction (which he himself approved of) and hastily write a short note in its place. We had worked over the book for so long that we were beginning to get fed-up. Nothing must be allowed to stand in the way of its immediate publication. When it appeared in 1936, bound and plainly jacketed, more like an elementary school book than a book of poetry, it received some good reviews from scholarly critics like F. K. Brown and W. F. Collin—Brown called its publication "the outstanding event in Canadian literature of the year"; but the public response was disappointing, only a small number of copies were sold, and John Sutherland, then in his communist phase, was able later to argue that the so-called 'Montreal-group' and Finch were out of touch with the common people and had little claim to significance in our mechanized and oppressive social system here and now.

Taking a longer view, it can be seen that *New Provinces* did have a considerable impact on the literary scene in Canada, as a number of later critics and literary historians, including Desmond Pacey in *Ten Canadian Poets*, Munro Beattie in the *Literary History of Canada* and Dudek and Gnarowski in *The Making of Modern Poetry in Canada* testify. Nevertheless, with the wisdom of hindsight I can see that the book could have been just that much better and more useful had we broadened even more the scope of our interest, and included some poems of Eustace Ross and Raymond Knister. Earle Birney's first poems in the *Canadian Forum*, of which he became literary editor in 1936, were just too late for us, but we ought to have taken something from Dorothy Livesay's *Signpost* of 1931. Then instead of the rather indifferent shorter poems of E. J. Pratt, how much stronger the book would have been had we persuaded him to let us use *The Cachalot*, his first masterpiece!

But in any case, *New Provinces* marked something of a break-through, at least for the four Montreal poets—Pratt had already made his. Acceptance by important American literary periodicals like *The Dial* and *Poetry* (Chicago) and the critical endorsements of Brown and Collin seemed to start us on our way. Then, sometime in 1939 or '40 I received an invitation to apply for a Guggenheim Fellowship—Frank Scott, my good angel, I think, had suggested my name. Casting about for a suitable research project it occurred to me that as I knew practically nothing about the historical development of a genuine Canadian poetry it would be a service both to myself and possibly my country to seek out the same and try to illustrate its characteristics from the point of view of a modern sensibility. A bold undertaking, no doubt, but a fascinating one. And when the Fellowship actually came through I set about it methodically and with enthusiasm.

On leave from the English Department at Michigan State, I spent the winter of 1941-42 in New York, reading Canadian poetry in the New York Public Library and hobnobbing with Ralph Gustafson, who was working on his Canadian anthology for Penguin, Leon Edel, an old friend from the *McGill Fortnightly* days, and Lew Schwartz, the dynamic business manager of the *Fortnightly*, at that time owner and editor of two trade journals, one the jewelry trade and the other the liquor business. In the spring I travelled across Canada, stopping mainly in Fredericton, Montreal, Toronto, and Vancouver, buying old Canadian poetry in second-hand book shops—at prices a very small fraction of what they would be today, and meeting everyone interested in Canadian literature—poets, critics, reviewers, or teachers. In Montreal there was the group that was about to found *Preview*, gathered around Frank Scott, a sort of father figure, and Patrick Anderson, including, among others, Pat Page, already giving promise of becoming the fine poet we know now, and A. M. Klein, whom I knew well. Irving Layton hovered on the periphery of the group, at that time, I think, an admirer and disciple of Klein.

But it was an extended visit to Toronto that proved most fruitful of all. I met E. J. Pratt for the first time, and at once any misunderstanding or disagreement we may have had over *New Provinces*—he had once written to Frank Scott, "Who is this man Smith?"—vanished. His unstinting kindly help was given with enthusiastic generosity, and we soon became good friends. Pelham Edgar and Northrop Frye also helped me, and I worked for long hours in the James Collection of Canadiana in the library of Victoria College, where Edgar, Pratt, and Frye were all teaching. Among the people of my own generation, most of them graduate students in English, who showed an interest in my project were Earle Birney, Ernest Sirluck, recently president of the University of Manitoba, Claude Bissell, who needs no introduction, and Paul Corbett, then of W. J. Gage and Company, who was to become an editor and first champion of the anthology Gage and the University of Chicago Press were later to publish jointly. Corbett introduced me to a young woman named Margaret Avison, who was working for Gage and living penuriously, chiefly on coffee. She showed me her poems in manuscript, and the fact that I was able to bring the anthology to a close with a selection of her poetry, almost the first to be published, I consider one of the real forward-looking achievements of the book.

In hours of relaxation we used to descend into the King Cole Room, a famous beverage room for Ladies with Escorts in the Park Plaza Hotel, "hard by", as one might say, the university. There one memorable evening I was introduced to a young undergraduate, who was too young to be legally served beer. He settled for ginger ale, which he sipped fastidiously. He was reputed to be brilliant, and though I don't think he had published any poetry, at that time perhaps not even written any, there was an impish, Puck-like spirit about him that looking back now I realize is characteristic of the author of *A Suit of Nettles*.

I don't know whether I met Jay Macpherson at this time, but certainly I did—years later—at the Kingston Conference of 1955. She was the only poet in Earle Birney's discussion group who admitted, as I had done in my address on "The Poet," to writing primarily for other poets.

Before leaving this account of my preparatory visit to Toronto I must recall one impressive scene. It was the final parade of the university Canadian Officers Training Corps, and with a certain apprehensive emotion a group of friends watched Lieutenants Birney, Bissell, Sirluck, and Corbett march off on the start of the long journey to Europe and eventually the war in France.

*The Book of Canadian Poetry* was published in 1943. Its aim was stated frankly and rather boldly at the beginning of the Introduction: "The main purpose of this collection is to illustrate in the light of a contemporary and cosmopolitan literary consciousness the broad development of English-Canadian poetry from its beginnings at the end of the eighteenth century to its renewal of power in the revolutionary world of today." I am afraid the claim to the possession of "a contemporary and cosmopolitan literary consciousness" offended the Victorian and patriotic prejudices of some Canadians. W. A. Deacon, dean of Toronto literary reviewers, led the attack on the whole modern movement in Canadian verse in the *Globe & Mail*. I can quote from it here because I have a copy of a letter, now in the Dominion Archives, I sent to A. M. Klein containing some excerpts from Deacon's very mixed and mixed-up review. He wrote, in part:

> Taken for what it is, this is an exceptionally fine, comprehensive and judicious piece work. . . . [But] the casual reader must not expect to find here the old favorites. A greater number of pages [than to the Roberts-Carman group] is accorded at the end to the poets of our surrealist school, including prominently A. J. M. Smith himself, . . . an attempt to popularise a group of highly mannered writers who make a cult of obscurity to the point that they have been unable as individuals to make any impression at all upon the reading public. . . . Professor Smith has won a fine bridgehead for the comrades that will permit them to infiltrate into university circles faster than they have been doing.
>
> We needed this book badly. It is an outright challenge to literary values in Canada and a healthy thing to have happened. If Duncan Campbell Scott cannot hold his own with A. M. Klein, Scott will have to go. . . . But Prof. Smith must remember that it is he who joined the battle: and if it should be his friend Klein who suffers, the loss must be where it falls.

After this nonsense I don't know how the reviewer could deviate into sense and think it consistent to end his article with the statement (possibly ironic?) "Prof. Smith has exhibited in his selections a taste, if at times severe, yet always sound."

In his reply to my letter, Klein commented that such stuff "added to the gaiety of nations. . . . The single impression I get," he added, "both from your facts and general mention elsewhere is that the Canadian Authors' Association and people of that ilk now know definitely that their day is done. In their reviews their spokesmen go through a resisting pantomime; but these are only the gestures of the moribund." Klein was also very scornful of a review by P. D. R. in the *Ottawa Journal* that accused him of writing 'free verse' and cited his poem "Autobiographical" as an example!

This shows something of the atmosphere of those days. "I never wrote a line of free verse in my life," he said. Deacon's review and Klein's comments might serve as a footnote to F. R. Scott's well-known satire, "The Canadian Authors Meet."

Unlike most of the newspaper reviews, those in the university quarterlies, like Frye's in the *Forum*, were serious and intelligent, though many were not without some critical reservations. Northrop Frye's review, or, rather, essay, was a general yet detailed examination of the whole anthology, its introduction, its organization, its inclusions and exclusions, and its probable influence. Even more important, it presented a theory of the nature and character of Canadian poetry in its broad development The heart of Frye's hypothesis can be stated succinctly in his own words: "According to Mr. Smith's book, the outstanding achievement of Canadian poetry is the evocation of stark terror."

Frye was to develop and illustrate this idea in two fine later essays, "Preface to an Uncollected Anthology" and "The Narrative Tradition in English-Canadian Poetry" reprinted in *The Bush Garden* (1971). It gave me an immense lift to find in the Preface to that book the statement that the 1943 anthology had first brought his interest in Canadian poetry into focus—I am quoting almost exactly—and given it direction, and "What it did for me it did for a great many others."

However gratifying such a tribute may be, it is perhaps more becoming of me to notice some of the critical reservations entertained by some other scholarly reviewers. Norman Endicott, for example, in a very fair-minded notice in The *Canadian Historical Review*, which began, "Maple leaves adorn with patriotic artlessness both the jacket and the cover of *The Book of Canadian Poetry*, but Mr. Smith's own introduction and selection in neither immature nor uncritical," went on to dismiss the satire and social comment of early versifiers like McLachlan and O'Grady as "not much above mere rhyme" and dismissed Charles Heavysege, "a poet of man not trees, no doubt, but to my mind singularly pseudo-Elizabethan and mediocre." He wished more space had been given to Lampman and (presumably) less to Crawford and Cameron. Coming to the moderns, after saying that the editor "is generous in his praise of individual poets and sensible in his attack on certain kinds of 'regionalism', he adds "I am not able to follow him in his very high estimate of the *general* technical brilliance of Canadian 'witty' or 'metaphysical' verse." Professor Endicott's point of view, which is perhaps more widely shared than I realized, is very different from the angry uniformed distaste of a W. A. Deacon.

One of the most interesting divergencies of opinion among the critics was on the worth of Heavysege. In my Introduction and biographical note, seduced by the wonderful passages I had managed to dig out of the vast rubble heap of *Saul* and two or three magnificent sonnets, I emphasised his virtues and underplayed his faults. I was not alone in this. Northrop Frye wrote: "In Charles Heavysege he has unearthed . . . a genuine Canadian Beddoes, a poet of impressive power and originality." Ralph Gustafson in *UTQ* spoke of Heavysege in similar terms—"a poet of power, originality, and, at times, majesty." He added. 'There is nothing comparable in the range of Canadian literature to Heavysege's creation, in *Saul*, of the character, Malzah." This last observation is true. A. M. Klein, in a long letter about the anthology, was another poet to praise Heavysege. This is not surprising for Klein himself has something akin to Heavysege, both in his great virtues and his occasional lapses. He wrote: "The man [Heavysege] had a Shakespearean scope. . . . With all their faults his sonnets are splendid things. I know no other sonneteer who has the faculty of so illuminating his fourteenth line. Only Don Jose Maria de Heredia wrote sonnets of the same kind, where the fourteenth line flips open like a fan, revealing the complete design." This is the testimony of a poet. It should not be dismissed lightly.

But neither should the scholarly discriminations of E. K. Brown in *On Canadian Poetry*, where both the faults and virtues of Heavysege are carefully recorded. "Here is a poet intoxicated with language," Brown noted. "*Saul* is cabinet-drama." It is dramatically ineffective. But this should not lead his modern detractors to deny his merits "as a realist, even as a bitter humorist" though a grotesque one. I myself would add now another, and perhaps, ambiguous virtue—his seemingly effortless power to write 'good' bad poetry. I shall limit myself to one illustration—a single line from Heavysege's pseudo-Jacobean 'dark' comedy, *Count Filippo*. The villain of the piece is addressing his sulky mistress, Paphiana:

> What, pouting Paph? Come, purr a
> little, Puss!

An exaltation of alliteration, indeed!

I have mentioned Professor Endicott's condemnation of Heavysege, and there were a good many others. Of them all John Sutherland's was the most vehement. After almost a page of rather heavy sarcasm at my expense—this is in his Introduction to *Other Canadians*—he concludes, "Anyway, who the devil would be interested enough in *Saul* to start offering 'explanations'?" Very much later Professor Millar, reviewing the *Oxford Book of Canadian Verse* in *The Tamarack Review* in 1960 could see no reason for taking Heavysege—" (lie heavy on him, earth') —seriously. (He also thought Lampman "a good old cheese.") George Woodcock wrote, more soberly, that "Victorian versifiers like Heavysege, Sangster, and Mair, were dead before they reached the grave.

However, the one really serious and fully developed attack on the 1943 anthology—not limited to the treatment of Heavysege at all—was, of course, John Sutherland's. I have not commented on this attack before. I will do so now. The advantage of hindsight makes it easier.

There is a very fair account of the controversy in Dudek and Gnarowski's *The Making of Modern Poetry in Canada*, and since they reprint Frye's long favorable review as well as Sutherland's attack, I have little to complain of. They distribute praise about equally to the two contestants—well, perhaps not quite equally. Sutherland's essay is called "a brilliant and prophetic piece of polemical writing, containing a sound core of critical argument. . . ." On the other hand: "Smith had written a capable and well-balanced Introduction—a progress report on Canadian poetry, when to his surprise he found he had unwittingly wandered into the middle of a battlefield. Poetry in Canada had moved forward since 1926, and Smith living in East Lansing, Michigan, was unaware that in Montreal at the moment two divergent parties were contesting the field."

This last sentence, of course, is ridiculous. I was certainly *not* unaware of the fact that poetry in Canada had moved forward since 1926. Practically all the poems in the last two Modern sections of *The Book of Canadian Poetry* had been written since 1926—most of them in the mid-thirties and a few in the very early forties. The "two divergent parties" referred to by Dudek and Gnarowski were the groups of poets who edited *Preview*, founded in 1942, and those about the same time who produced *First Statement*. The first group might be considered the 'cosmopolitan.' The second—the 'native' or, better, the proletarian—included Sutherland as editor and Irving Layton and Louis Dudek as influential contributors. It was, I think, the division of the modern part of the anthology into Native and Cosmopolitan that mainly irritated Sutherland. The poets in the Native category somehow felt cheated; subconsciously they wanted to be classed with the Cosmopolitans as somehow more sophisticated and knowing, and this feeling was to break out in the rivalry between the two magazines, which officially at least, came to an end with the merging of *Preview* and *First Statement* in 1945 as *Northern Review*, under the triumphant leadership of John Sutherland as editor.

Sutherland had originally taken a more tolerant view of the native and cosmopolitan split, which, I must note, clearly exists in American poetry as well as Canadian. Consider Whitman, Sandburg, Vachel Lindsay, and William Carlos Williams on the one hand and Wallace Stevens, Eliot, Pound, and Marianne Moore, on the other. In an editorial in *First Statement* for February 1944 Sutherland had written: "Smith in the introduction to his *Book of Canadian Poetry* makes a distinction between a 'native' and a 'cosmopolitan' tradition. . . . I don't know whether this distinction has been made before, but it is a valuable one and it throws a good deal of light on Canadian poetry. But are the characteristics of the two traditions correctly defined? Can Mr. Smith ignore the colonialism that stamps the work of Canadian poets, particularly writers of the cosmopolitan group? As his scholarly and well-balanced anthology makes abundantly clear" —I quote these words to show John Sutherland's fundamentally generous and honest approach—no poetry movement in Canada has ever taken place that did not depend, in the matter of style, upon the example of a previous movement in some other country."

This is true, but it does not follow that to enter into the stream of international European and American poetry and to go to school to Pound or Eliot, or Baudelaire, Yeats, or Auden is to be merely colonial. I must add, in all fairness, that Sutherland also asserts that "those modern poets who continued the native tradition also waited for the go-ahead signal to come from England and America." No one denies that there has been a time-lag—accounted for, I think, by our small and thinly scattered population and the tough and rugged natural background that Frye makes so much of, but this is not to condemn *all* Canadian poets, modern and Victorian alike, as mere colonials, and if carried forward to the immediate present would dismiss the

poets of the *Tish* school and many of the best of our contemporaries like Newlove or Bowering as well as Souster's *New Wave*
school as imitators of Williams or Olson, Creeley or Gary Sny-
der—not Canadians at all but colonials of the U.S.

At the time Sutherland was engaged in these polemics he was
a dedicated Marxist, and this led him to have a great deal of
rather heavy-handed fun at the expense of what he mistook for
my religious bias: "Mr. Smith is a classicist by inclination, a
Catholic by intention, and a Royalist by what he will certainly
achieve . . . " and this accounted for my good opinion of Heavysege!

When Sutherland was converted to Catholicism and broke
with his left-wing followers, Layton and Dudek, he made a very
handsome, almost noble, recantation. In an essay on "The Past
Decade in Canadian Poetry," written at the end of the forties, he
wrote, "I criticized Mr. Smith for his religious emphasis"—an
emphasis that was surely in Sutherland's mind alone—"and I
protested that his effort to force a religious interpretation on the
new poets was not abiding by the rules and prophesied that it
would prove futile. Well, I take it back. I still think Mr. Smith
was forcing matters at that time, but the event has shown that he
was substantially right. For the new poets have come back, if not
always to religion, at least to a soul-searching which has strong
religious implications." This is honest and forthright, as Sutherland always was, but I cannot think what poets he had in mind.

As I began to think about the preparation of a second edition
of *The Book of Canadian Poetry* I came to realize that the twofold division of the modern poets was more confusing than helpful. In which category, for example, should Earle Birney go? or
Dorothy Livesay? In both, obviously, but impossibly. It had
been Northrop Frye who pointed out the truth. He remarked
somewhere that while the division between native and cosmopolitan is a real one, it does not exist clear-cut in Canadian
poetry as a whole; it is a division in the mind and heart of each
individual poet. This was the solution to the problem. I should
have seen it for myself. I eliminated the division from the subsequent edition, and I think everyone approved.

After the success of the Canadian poetry anthology it seemed
only natural to begin a study of our prose literature, and in 1945
I was given a Rockefeller grant for two years to travel in Canada
and begin such a study. This time I met and talked chiefly with
novelists. I have very happy memories of the kindness I received
from Theodore Roberts in Digby, Nova Scotia, Morley Callaghan, whom I already knew, in Toronto, W. O. Mitchell in
High River, Alberta, and Ethel Wilson, Malcolm Lowry, and

Howard O'Hagan, my old Editor-in-Chief from the *McGill Daily* days, in Vancouver. You will see how hard I worked on this project, as Stephen Leacock might have put it, when you realize that the first volume of *The Book of Canadian Prose*, now retitled *The Colonial Century*, did not appear until 1965, twenty years after, and the much larger second volume, *The Canadian Century*, until 1973. But such procrastination was actually all to the good. The book was able to include selections from the writers of the explosive fifties and sixties—material well worth waiting for.

In the mid-forties and early fifties I was also working on two non-Canadian anthologies. One, *Seven Centuries of Verse—English and American*, was a college text published by Charles Scribner's Sons in 1947 and revised and updated in 1957 and 1967; the other was a collection of what I called 'serious light verse' from Chaucer and Skelton to Auden and L. A. Mackay. It was called *The Worldly Muse* and was published by Abelard Press in 1951. The press was owned by the late Lew Schwartz, who had been the energetic business manager of the *McGill Fortnightly Review*. Unlike the very successful college text, *The Worldly Muse* had bad luck from the start, and six months or so after its publication almost the entire stock was destroyed in a warehouse fire. A couple of brief but favorable reviews in *The New Yorker* and *The New Republic* and notices in scattered newspapers in Canada and the U.S. were all I saw. A few of my friends have copies of the book, and they tell me it is a delightful bedside companion.

*The Worldly Muse*, however, did serve me in good stead when, three or four years later, I began working on a second collaboration with Frank Scott that was to result in the publication of *The Blasted Pine: An Anthology of Satire, Invective, and Disrespectful Verse Chiefly by Canadian Writers*. This was in 1957, with a second updated edition ten years later. The original urge to collect such a body of material was Frank's, and I fell in with the idea with enthusiasm. I had a good deal of material left over from the big anthology and was glad of the opportunity to illustrate the popular local poetry of low life and the crude but lively political polemics, as well as the amusing light verse of our modern 'university wits' like L. A. Mackay and F. R. Scott himself. The greater part of the earlier inclusions were found by me, I think, and the later by Frank. I wrote the Introduction, but it was submitted to my collaborator sentence by sentence as it was being composed, and we worked it over with a fine-tooth comb just as we used to do nearly thirty years before with editorials for the *McGill Fortnightly*.

When we had most of the manuscript ready the problem of

arrangement was before us. We gathered the sheafs of unnumbered pages in a heap and began to shuffle them around and pile them up on the floor of Frank's living room on Clarke Avenue, Westmount, sorting them into groups. Then came the difficult and chancy job of finding titles for the various sections. I believe it was I—I had had a lot of practice at this sort of thing when compiling *The Wordly Muse*—who finally came up with most of them. Kildare Dobbs, our Macmillan editor, had already made up his own list and stashed it away in case we should get stuck. We never saw his list, but it was a comfort to know it was there. The notes we wrote in the closest collaboration. We had researched the facts in about equal proportion, and we wrote them up, one of us sitting at the typewriter and the other striding up and down dictating, with a sentence by the dictator (often after a long pause for discussion) being amended, or completed, or entirely recast by the man at the machine.

As long ago as 1942 in a survey of Canadian anthologies published in the *University of Toronto Quarterly* I had castigated the puerilities of Wilfred Campbell's *Oxford Book of Canadian Verse* of 1913.* In justification I will only repeat—and for comic relief as well—a verse from one of the poems included in Campbell's anthology. It is from the description of a pure and innocent maiden by Charles Mair.

> Beneath her sloping neck.
> Her bosom-gourds swelled chastely,
>     white as spray,
>         Wind-tost—without a fleck—
> The air which heaved them was
>     less pure than they.

At the end of the discussion of the 1913 *Oxford Book* I had written, "A revision is badly needed."

It was not until the fifties were drawing to a close that this became a possibility. I began pestering my friends Ivon Owen and William Toye, who were then in editorial command at the Canadian Oxford Press, to let me try and, rather to my surprise, they succeeded in persuading the Delegates of the Press in England to do just that. I think it was perhaps my suggestion that the book should include an ample selection of French-Canadian poetry in French that turned the trick.

I set to work at once with an ethusiasm that recalled the first days of my Canadian diggings in 1941. I knew the English po-

---

*Included in this volume.

etry pretty well by now, of course, but I had to start from scratch
with the French. I read first the old standard comprehensive
*Anthologie des Poètes Canadiens* of 1920 by Jules Fournier and
the modern *Anthologie de la Poésie Canadienne Française* of
Guy Sylvestre, with whom I corresponded and who gave me the
benefit of his critical acumen. I bought the collected poems of
Fréchette, Nelligan, DesRochers, Choquette, and Saint-Denys-
Garneau, and the various volumes of Alain Grandbois, Anne
Hébert, and the younger poets of Hexagon and *Parti Pris*. I read
these—or perhaps I should say read *in* them—aided occasionally
by a dictionary and sometimes by my old friend and master-
translator John Glassco. I also sought out all available English
translations, particularly those of Gael Turnbull and, of course,
Frank Scott. The results seem to have been successful, and there
were few if any complaints, either about the proportions—one-
third of the poems included were in French—or the choices
themselves.

As far as the English side of the anthology was concerned, it
was a refining and concentrating (and a little updating) of *The
Book of Canadian Poetry*. As I have not changed my view of the
over-all development and nature of Canadian poetry, the long
Introduction is also not other than a refining and concentrating,
perhaps with a few new insights, of the introduction to the earlier
book. The account of the French poetry was, needless to say,
entirely new.

The Canadian reviews were all that I could wish, but I must
admit I was disappointed with the English. The few that I saw
were mostly condescending and superior. I am disappointed too
that after a second printing the hard-cover edition in the traditional blue-and-gold uniform of the Oxford Books of Verse was
allowed to go out of print—hastened, I believe, by the purchase
of two hundred copies by External Affairs for distribution to
embassies and libraries abroad. The paperback edition, with its
rather gaudy *nouveau-art* cover is still flourishing.

The *Oxford Book* was fortunate in being able to include sam-
ples of the very fine body of work produced by Canadian poets
in the fifties, though the astonishing creative explosion of poetry
in the sixties had to wait (for a partial representation at least)
until 1967, when I was able to persuade the Oxford Press to let
me do not what would have been preferable, an updating of
*OBCV*, but a new book, *Modern Canadian Verse in English and
French*.

The Canadian and American reviews of the modern book
were good, but the one which pleased me most was a French one

by the Montreal critic Jean Ethier-Blais in *Le Devoir*. While, like many of his compatriots, Blais did not quite approve of paring off English and French poems in the same volume, he wrote most generously of the French selections. "Qui a guidé Professeur Smith dans son choix des oeuvres de langue française? Personne, semble-t-il, sinon lui-même. Pour ma part, je trouve ce choix parfait. . . . " What more could an anthologist ask? I should add that the kind of assistance I received from friends like John Glassco and Guy Sylvestre were with difficult points of translation or questions of the general reputation of various poets in the French literary community. The actual choices were my own.

But it is time to turn to something more fundamental. I believe every critic, and certainly every anthologist, should examine his own position in relation to every poet he is concerned with. I want to know whether I have discovered the principles that guide me inductively by the examination and analysis of many poems or whether I have made certain assumptions and then found poems to sustain them.

I hope the former.

In working on an anthology my practice has always been to read as many poems as possible and to choose those that strike me as most appropriate to the purpose in hand—to illustrate in the Canadian collections the variety and growth of poetry in Canada. But the nature of that variety and the stages of its growth—these will be defined and determined by the consideration of the poems. Perhaps this is to tackle two ends of the problem at once, but it works.

This process, when fruitful, begins with a sudden flash of recognition, a sudden onrush of pleasure—the emotional sources of critical insights are sometimes as significant as those of poetry. Reading, say, through the poems of Roberts I come on this in a little six-line poem called "Ice";

> The water shrank, and shuddered,
>     and stood still—

or in a sonnet entitled "The Mowing"—

> The crying knives glide on;
>     the green swath lies,

and I feel something akin to what Lampman felt on that November day when he came on a field of dead mulleins—

> And shuddering between cold and heat,
> Drew my thoughts closer, like a cloak,
> While something in my blood awoke,

A nameless and unnatural cheer, —
A pleasure secret and austere.

Such brief flashes as these are certainly 'Canadian', certainly 'native'. But the more complex myth-making imagination we find in Isabella Valancy Crawford, Pratt, and Birney, or in the Emily Carr sonnet of Wilfred Watson—is common enough in our literature to suggest that this is one of the most powerful results of the special ardours and grandeurs of our northern environment. When, however, we turn to the brief objective 'laconics' of Eustace Ross or many of the poems of Raymond Souster, we learn that there is another and different aspect of our native poetry—a simplicity and *naiveté*, a sort of innocence of eye and heart, that instinctively avoids rhetoric and metaphor alike—a characteristic I would rather call *modesty* than *timidity*.

Ross, who, it seems to have been forgotten, was represented and highly praised in the first of the Canadian anthologies in 1943, wrote with a simple and beautifully unassuming clarity of such overlooked but immensely significant things as—

the creek, shining
out of the deep woods

moving between banks
crowded with raspberry bushes

or

The white gum showing
in the gloom
along the massive
trunk of a great
pine-tree standing
on the hill
with a deep bed
of needles below

or

The snake trying
to escape the pursuing stick
           How beautiful
and graceful are his shapes!

he vanishes in the ripples
among the green reeds.

This is perhaps a North American note, not exclusively a Canadian one—surely as native to the woods around Paterson, New Jersey as to those around Toronto or Ottawa. Yet there is a sort of graceful diffidence about them—as sometimes in the poetry of Souster and occasionally in Purdy—that seems to me more in keeping with the spirit of Canada—or maybe only of Ontario—than with that of the more aggressive and self-confident United States.

In any case, it is well worth noting and preserving.

# THE NEW CANADIAN LIBRARY LIST